Baby, it's cold outside. I released th

Because, I love yo

MW00466332

# OLIVIA GAINES

# BLIND
# HOPE

HE KEPT HIS PROMISE, BUT SHE HELD HIS HOPE.

COTTER WIHLBORG MADE a promise that he intended to keep. He kept his word to Caleb Morrow to take the sealed box home to the dying man's wife and kid, arriving to find both in dire straits. The house was in shambles, the cupboards were bare and the widow was on death's door. Nursing her back to health, Cotter found himself falling in love with the land, the kid and also the woman. Both he and the widow had a secret, leaving them clinging to a blind hope, that each would find forgiveness for sins unspoken.

# Blind Hope

**JANUARY 30, 2019**
DAVONSHIRE HOUSE PUBLISHING
Augusta, Georgia

## The Technicians- Book 2

# OLIVIA GAINES

# Chapter One – The Promise

It was colder than the nipples on an ugly, wart-faced witch with three tits. Even with the heat on full blast, Cotter Wihlborg couldn't seem to get warm. He didn't know where in the hell Rocheport, Missouri was and based on his current feelings, right now he didn't really give a damn. What he did care about was the promise he made to a dying man, and come high tides during a Monsoon, keeping his word meant a thing or two to him. Freezing his balls off meant a thing or two to him as well since at some point, he planned to settle down and have a few crumb snatchers with a big butt woman that he liked to call Babe as he fondled her large breast.

He didn't have a Babe. It had been so long since he'd bedded a woman, the lady at the gas station with three teeth looked like a good time to him. He blew warms puffs of air into his nearly frozen fisted hands, trying desperately to warm his fingers before jamming them into the front pockets of his jeans. Never one to use credit cards, he went inside the smelly station, grabbing bags of chips, a browning banana, and a couple bottles of electrolyte replacers, and he settled his tab. Additionally, he purchased four cans of soup just in case he couldn't find a decent place to eat later this evening. Behind the counter, a crater-faced woman grinned at him, saying something in a country version of English he barely understood, but the gleam in her eye said enough. The way the semi-white pegs dangled from her gums, were far enough apart to give a thirsty man a place to park his horse. A horny horse. A horse that had been out to pasture for entirely too long and in dire need of a pretty filly to warm his hooves.

"Thanks, Liz," he said as he read her name tag.

"My name ain't Liz. The last girl that had the job, this was her name tag," she said, grinning at him again. "I'm just wearing it 'til Vernon gets me a new one."

He didn't know Vernon. The silly woman didn't bother to tell him her actual name and he didn't really give two horns on a bull either way. She raised her eyebrows at him in that knowing manner, and even as much as he wanted a warm socket to stick his wrench, that hole would probably give him an incurable rash.

"Thanks, either way," he said, collecting his change. "Have a good night."

The brim of his baseball hat sat low across his brow as he turned up the collar on the old sheepskin lined leather jacket and headed for his car. The tank, now filled with gas, allowed him to pump up the heat and tunes as he motored his way back to I-70, headed west towards the small town and homestead where Caleb Morrow said he had a ranch. He also said he had a wife and kid. His last wish was for Cotter to take home the metal box.

Curiosity had killed enough cats in Cotter's line of work, and the last thing he wanted or planned to do, was open the box to see what was inside. He'd given his word to Caleb that he would deliver the box to the ranch just outside of Rocheport, and that he planned to do. If he just knew where the fuck the place was. The town barely showed up on a map, let alone the Morrow Farms.

Through the speaker of the car, the British accent of his GPS navigator told him in five hundred feet, to take exit 115 to Hwy Bb.

"Fuck," he muttered. "This town is so small the roads have alphabets and not numbers."

Taking the exit, he followed the sexy British voice up the pitch-dark highway, using his high beams just in case a deer bolted out and decided to become a hood ornament on his truck. It didn't take long to reach Rocheport, and even less time to drive through the hiccup the locals called a town. Highway Bb turned into Third Street which lasted all of seven blocks and dead-ended on a road with options to turn left or right. The GPS said go right, turning onto Highway 240 which took him across Moniteau Creek.

Cotter knew he was close to the place since Caleb had said that's where he and his family got most of their water. For two days, he listened to the man tell him about his little piece of the American pie. A sustainable ranch, off the grid, with solar power, a living roof, and hot water piped in from the solar arrays which rotated to catch the rays of sun. Truth be told, Cotter wanted to see the place. At the next road, he made a left onto Highway 440 which took him a mile before the British sidekick coming through his speakers said take the next left.

"You have arrived at your destination," the voice said.

"The hell you say," Cotter shouted. It was a dark road with a broken-down fence. The high beams back up, he drove up the dirt road, looking for signs of life. The splintered fencing was just the start of the problems he could see in the darkened pathway as he crept his way to the house. A sole light shone through a dirty window. The fireplace billowed no smoke and the house all but appeared deserted.

He cut the truck's engine and slowly opened the door. His black boots stood out against the white snow as they crunched in the soft dusting of flakes where his feet had just landed. The blood in his veins pumped fiercely as he made his way to the broken wooden steps, having to step over the middle one, which held a large crack. The porch itself were splintered planks of wood. When he raised his hand to knock on the door, it swung open. A sallow-eyed boy, of no more than six, opened the door.

"Daddy!" the kid yelled.

"No, I'm not your Pa, but he did send me," Cotter said.

"Who is it, Johnnie? Who's there?" a weak woman's voice said.

"A man. He said Daddy sent him," the child said, opening the door for Cotter to enter. His eyes adjusted, and the dim light he'd seen from the window was a kerosene heater, on its last ounces of juice. They were warming themselves by its pitiful heat.

"Hello," the woman said, trying to sit up. The pallid color of her skin, along with the dry cracked lips, indicated the woman was sick. The kid was skin and bones and the place was freezing.

"You have any firewood?" Cotter asked.

"Too weak to cut anymore," the woman said. The smell of her sickness filled the air and he knew the stench of death was hovering around the frail body waiting to take its toll.

"Where do you keep the wood?"

"Out back," the kid said. "I brought in all the ones I could, but then the snow came. I wasn't strong enough to carry the big ones or lift the ax to cut any."

"Close this door. I'll be back," Cotter said, heading out the front door. He went to his truck and grabbed a few blankets, taking them back inside the house and giving one to the kid, who acted as if he'd just brought in pizza and The Emoji's movie. The woman, he swaddled in the second on before going out the door again.

Pulling his thick leather work gloves from the compartment of the truck, he also threw a heavy scarf around his neck and grabbed a flashlight. Making his way around the back of the house, he located the pile of wood by accidentally stumbling over it. If this is what they called a pile, then it was going to be a long night. Gratefully, the wood was covered in a tarp which had kept it dry for the most part. Grabbing the largest logs from the bottom of the stack, his arms quivered from the weight as he carried them inside the house. Dumping them by the fireplace, he knelt, looking for kindling and found none.

"Crap," he said, trying to look around for paper or anything to get the fire started. Stomping back to his truck, he picked up the newspaper he'd purchased in St. Louis, pissed that he hadn't had a chance to read it, and definitely wouldn't now, as he marched back into the house, shredding the paper and stuffing it around the logs. Using his trusty flint lighter, he held the flame to the edges of the paper, waiting for it to catch fire. With the knife, which he kept in his pocket, Cotter chipped away at a log, breaking off smaller pieces, sticking it in between the wood.

The room began to warm as the logs started to burn, and he knew it wouldn't be enough to keep them warm all night. A loud rumbling from the boy's stomach reverberated through the room as he looked about the sorrowful place, awakening under the light from the fire. Caleb had lied. The house was a shithole and he left this woman and child in it to rot as he traipsed about, eating in fine restaurants while they sat in a shack, dying of God only knew what.

"Mister, did you bring any food?" the boy asked, "Me and Ma hadn't had anything to eat in a while, and we're mighty hungry."

"Sure, does the stove work?"

"Naw," he said. "It needs wood too."

"Stay close by the fire, be right back," Cotter said, heading out the door again. "Damn you, Caleb Morrow!"

From his truck, he grabbed the food supplies he'd gotten at the filling station, along with two more logs of wood that he carried inside. He could almost hear the boy licking his lips as he shoved a log into the old cookstove, adding more of his damned newspaper that he wouldn't get to read, along with more chips of the wood.

"Where's the pots, son?"

"Over the stove," the boy said.

Two pots. Both dirty. Reaching for the light switch, he flipped it and nothing happened. Going to the sink, he turned the nob, and again nothing happened.

"We ran out of water a day or two ago," the boy said. "I think the well's frozen."

"No worries," Cotter said as he opened a bottle of water, pouring some into a glass for the kid and a bit into a mug for the woman. "Give your mother some water. Let her sip it slowly."

"Yes sir," the boy said, sipping his own, then helping his mother. The remainder of water in the bottle he used to wash the pot, rinse it, and open two cans of soup. He heated it over the woodburning stove, watching it bubble, before ladling the contents into two bowls.

"That sure smells good," the boy said. "I'm Johnnie Morrow. This is my Ma, Judy. You said my Daddy sent you?"

"He did Johnnie," Cotter said.

"Is he coming home soon? He's sure been gone a long time," Johnnie said, accepting the bowl of soup.

"No son, he won't be coming back anytime soon," Cotter said, walking over to Judy. "Mrs. Morrow, can you sit up and eat?"

She shook her head no.

"I'm going to check you for fever. Is there anything I should know before reaching over there?" Cotter asked.

"I think it's pneumonia," she whispered.

Touching her forehead, it was hot to the coolness of his fingertips. "Yeah, you are burning up. Let's break that fever and give you some fluids to get you upright, and then we'll worry about healing those lungs."

"You a doctor, Mister?" Johnnie asked, eyeballing the second bowl of soup that Cotter had prepared for his mother, but now passed to him.

"No, but I'm going to see about getting your Mother better," he said.

"Is she gonna die?"

"Not on my watch," Cotter said, taking the blanket from Johnnie and wrapping Judy in another layer. He moved her body, which felt frail compared to carrying the heavy logs of wood to the floor in front of the fire. He braced her back against the smooth stones, hoping the heat from the fire had warmed them enough to penetrate the soggy lungs in her chest.

Slowly reaching for the cup, he put it to the dry, cracked lips, urging her to drink. After taking a few sips, he went to his bag to retrieve the electrolyte water. "Mister, is there any more soup?"

"When was the last time you ate son?"

"I dunno, we had some crackers a day or so ago," Johnnie said.

"That's enough for tonight. Let's allow you little body to digest what you just ate, and in the morning, I will see about getting some food in this...place," he said, turning back to Judy. He held the cup up to her lips again, almost forcing the lime green color liquid down her throat.

"Thank you," she whispered. "You came just in time, I was barely holding on. The phone's dead. No car, he just left us here. Left us here to die."

"No, he didn't," Cotter lied. "He sent me."

Judy's eyes closed as if for the first time, since forever, she could actually sleep. He sat watching her. The brown skin, dry for lack of water, seemed thin across her cheekbones. The skin across her throat was gaunt like her face and eyes sunken as if she were only waiting for help to come for the boy so she could leave this world and he not be alone.

He hated Caleb Morrow even more so now than he had a week ago. This shit was unfair, not only to him but the boy and woman. Caleb had sent him here to rescue the family he'd abandoned.

In his heart, he wanted to dump them on the doorstep of the nearest hospital and let social services find a home for the boy. Caleb knew he wouldn't do that. Part of the reason the man didn't come home was because of him. For a year, he was hot on Caleb's trail, never giving the jack-hole a moment of peace, and a week ago, he had caught up with him.

A week ago, he put a bullet in the man.

A week ago, he watched Caleb Morrow bleed out into a slow death.

Caleb only asked him to do one thing, bring the box to his wife and kid. It pissed him off that Caleb made him promise he would. The reputation Cotter held in those outlying dark circles of the fringes of society meant everything to the man people hired to fix problems. Caleb had been a problem to someone and The Company sent Cotter to fix it.

"Out of the frying pan and into this fire," he mumbled, taking off his jacket. Looking around for a place to sleep, he got to his feet and searched for a bed to rest his head. The bedroom door was blocked at the bottom, and he pushed hard to get it open, only to find the room was colder than outside. The big hole in the roof was the cause of that.

"Be right back," he said, closing the door and going back to his truck to collect a few items. He came back with a sleeping bag that he put on the floor in front of the fire. Double checking the doors and windows to make sure they were locked, he kicked off his boots. To Judy he said, "You, sleeping bag, me, couch."

In his hand he held two pill bottles. He took a couple of pills from one, and one pill from the other. Sticking two tablets in her mouth, he made her drink and swallow the tablets. He added another pill between the cracked lips, giving more of the lemon-lime drink and then tucking Judy into the sleeping bag. He took one of the blankets away from her for the boy to sleep on near the fire before he threw his jacket over his chest as he settled on the too short couch.

"Mister?" Johnnie said.

"Not now son, I need some sleep. We will make a plan in the morning," Cotter said, leaning his head into the pillow and closing his eyes. "Ain't shit I can do tonight anyway."

# Chapter Two – Supplies

The sun had barely broken through the clouds when Cotter put on his boots and stomped around the back of the home, bringing the last of the firewood to the front porch and into the house. One log he put in the fireplace to get it started on keeping the room warm, the second he used in the cookstove, which also heated up the place as he warmed two more bowls of soup. It wasn't the best breakfast, but it was all they had for now.

Cotter eyeballed the kid, as he stood over him, tapping at his leg with the toe of his boot. Johnnie stirred, looking up at him. "I heated some soup for you and your Mom. I need you to feed it to her, even if she doesn't want it," he said.

"Are you leaving us?" Johnnie inquired, the large brown eyes filled with fear.

"Naw, gotta head to town for supplies. Get some more firewood, the well has to get going, and the hole in the roof needs to be patched," he told the kid.

"There's a hole in the roof in my room too," Johnnie said. "The dirt on the roof is too heavy with the snow. It fell in. Ma said it wasn't safe for me to get up there."

"Your Mother was right," Cotter said. "Be back soon."

He lifted Judy from the floor, placing her weakened body on the couch. "Headed to town. I'll try to make it quick. You need to eat and drink today. I can't play nursemaid so if you got any fight left in you, here is where it needs to kick in," he said in a stern voice.

Judy nodded her head in agreement. Her resolve seemed stronger this morning and it was enough to get him moving out the door. His head filled with questions, but there was so much wrong in the whole damned situation that the little bit of right inside of him needed to make sure they were okay before he left to go back to his own home in Venture, Georgia. A home he hadn't seen for year, chasing down the rogue contract on Caleb Morrow.

Anger coursed through him as he grabbed his keys and went out the front door. He hated the man with a passion for more reasons than the two he left inside that ramshackle of a house he called a home. Cotter was missing his own home and the comfort of his bed. Until he'd completed the contract on Caleb, The Company wouldn't give him any more jobs. The year he chased the elusive snake was a whole year that he had no income coming into his coffers. Now, he was going to have to spend a great deal of his personal dough to fix up the raggedy ass house. Even after sending proof of job completion, because it had taken so long to get the assignment done, the bonus attached to the contract was null and void. A lousy $50,000 job had cost him nearly half as much to get it done.

"Bastard! If you were still alive, I would shoot you again and watch you suffer," he mumbled as he started his truck and drove into the small town of Rocheport. The town offered eight places to eat and nary a one with supplies to fix a shitter. He took a parking spot in front of a small diner, wandering inside and looking for an old timer. Over the years on the job, he'd learned if you buy an old man a cup of coffee then ask them one question, they will tell you anything you need to know and some things you didn't. Squinting his eyes, he looked about the place for such a body. Bingo! Target acquired, he sat next to the old man on a stool at the counter.

"Coffee, sausage and egg sandwich on toast to go, please," Cotter told the girl behind the counter. "Morning Old Timer."

The watery ancient eyes that were blue at one point in the old man's life, but now just glazed over in cataracts, looked at him. "Who you calling Old Timer?"

"No disrespect, but I was looking for a place to snag some groceries and building materials," he said. "Got a little place up the road a bit, and it is colder here than a Georgia boy is used to, need some firewood and to patch a hole in my roof."

"You want a real grocery store or a make-do?"

"A make-do will help, but if I can do one trip to get the food, supplies, and firewood, it could save me a heck of a lot of energy that I'm gonna need to patch that roof and unfreeze my well," he said with honesty. "Can't go cooking in the pot without any water to wash down the potatoes."

The waitress brought over his sandwich and the cup of coffee to go. His stomach growled like a bear poked during hibernation since he didn't eat supper. Cotter took a big bite out of the sandwich, chewing quickly to ease the pain in his gut.

"Backwards or forwards, it's the same distance to Boonville or Columbia. Both are about 15 minutes from here," he said. "Columbia is a better bet, got themselves a Walmart over yonder plus the ABC supply store to get everything you need to fix the roof, well, and toilet."

"Thanks, you've been a big help," he said to the old man and placed a 20 on the counter.

"Mister, you don't want to wait for your change?" the waitress called out.

"No, that's for my stuff and his breakfast as well," he said, holding the cup of black coffee up to the old man. The man gave Cotter a nod, and Cotter made his way back to his truck. Sipping on the hot black coffee, he thought about the skinny boy and the sick woman as he gulped down the rest of his breakfast. Obeying the speed limits in Rocheport, he gave the truck some gas when he reached the outskirts of town. His anger spurring him on to the interstate and he merged into traffic towards Columbia.

The shopping took the better part of two hours, but he got everything he needed, including electric heat tape to unfreeze the heads of the well pump. Growing up in Minnesota, he knew a great deal about cold weather, which is why he had moved to Georgia. He hated the cold more than anything he could think of, and being in Missouri in the dead of December only pissed him off more.

In the bed of his truck was a load of firewood, wood to repair the roof and enough groceries to last two weeks. He'd purchased stew meats, a couple of whole chickens, and 12 bags of different types of dried beans along with yeast, flour, sugar, cornmeal, eggs and milk. A couple of containers of frozen concentrated juices, peanut butter, oatmeal and jam would do the trick to get the woman on her feet and some fat on the kid. His mother, God rest her soul, could make a meal out of the most basic items which kept him, his sister, and his brother with full bellies even in the scarcest of times. It was in his adult years at college when he first ate fast food. Never caring for the taste of processed easy gut fillers, he tended to veer away from it, but the brightly lit golden arches made him stop at the drive through for a kid's meal with extra fries and ketchup for the boy.

"Sucker," he mumbled to himself as he drove back to the homestead from hell. In the daylight, it looked worse than it did at night. The living roof, which is supposed to be covered in vegetation that Caleb boasted about was a bunch of dead plants stuck in mud on top of the house. The whole purpose of the roof was to provide insulation and drain off the rainwater. Between the weight of the dirt and the snow, he understood why the roof gave way in both rooms. "Today, just repair the holes, get the well going, and get fluids and food into them."

Johnnie was at the door when he drove up. The jeans he wore were too short and as cold as it was, the boy only had on a pair of socks riddled with holes. "Boy, put on a coat and some boots and come bring some of this firewood into the house," he said in a loud voice.

"My shoes are too small and I don't have a coat," he said. "Well I do, but it's too little."

"Get the shoes on and borrow your Mother's coat," Cotter said.

"Yes sir!" the boy said, closing the door. Moments later he was outside, the coat dragging the ground as he walked. The unruly head of curly hair hung from under the skull cap as he made his way to the truck, damned near tiptoeing in the boots that were too small for his feet. The small gloved hands reached into the bed of the truck, carrying as many cuts of wood as he could, placing a few in the fireplace right away. Others, he added to the stove, returning to unload the food and anything else his hands could carry.

Satisfied that he'd helped, Cotter handed him the kid's meal with the cup of orange pop. "For me?" Johnnie said in delight.

"Eat up. We have work to do," he said to the boy. Looking at Judy, he spoke softly, "How you feeling?"

"Found my fight," she said.

"Good enough," he told her, washing his hands with the bottle of water and spreading peanut butter on a slice of bread. "Try to eat this."

Her scant meal was accompanied by a cup of hot tea that she held between both hands.

"Gotta unfreeze the well, repair the roof, and warm up that bedroom so I can put you in bed. If I can get the power back on today, I will, but not making any promises," he said.

"I appreciate all of this," she whispered.

"Again, no promises," he cautioned. He hefted a five-gallon jug of water on-to his shoulders and took it into the bathroom. He refused to lift the toilet seat, but added water to the reservoir, filling the tank enough to give the toilet a flush. Loving the sound of the greedy toilet gurgling down the contents, he added more water.

On the back porch, he located a large tub where he loaded in the bags of ice he'd purchased and dropped in the meat. Calling for the boy through the back door, he told him, "Johnnie, when you're done eating, I need you to put clean snow on top of that meat, then set the gallon of milk on top of the snow. Understand?"

"Yes sir," the boy said, stuffing a french fry into his mouth.

Tamping down the snow on the tub, Cotter made his way inside the house to the kitchen where he opened a bag of pinto beans, placing the beans in a bowl and covering the dry beans with water. He'd let that soak for the rest of the day and into the night, and tomorrow, he'd put them on to slow cook all day. Sighing loudly, he made his way back outside and secured his toolbelt from the truck and then he strode off to locate a ladder, shovel, and rope. Tying the rope around the roof, he let the free end drop to the ground to wrap around the wood he'd use to repair the hole. He'd come back to that after he located the well, which wasn't difficult to find.

On his knees in the snow, he removed the wellhead cover, using the heating tape, wrapping it, and covering it with insulation. That would take a while to defrost, so he went to work on the roof. He patched, hammered, nailed, and put new shingles over the wood. Using the shovel, he scraped off the densest portions of dirt and snow to prevent another cave in. Standing on the roof, he looked over the land. The frozen creek ran behind the house a ways down the property, and sure enough, if his eyes could believe it, was the solar array Caleb had mentioned. Cotter made his way off the roof and down the ladder. His tool belt hanging loosely about his hips, he went to the solar array.

He checked the connecting lines to the pivoting panels, tracing the cords through the snow until he found the break in the line. "Asshole didn't bother to bury the cables," he grunted, pushing away snow. He cleared the lines all the way to the house and located the battery assembly. Disconnecting all of the batteries, Cotter went back to the break. Using his snipping tools, he cut away the frayed edges, stripping back the plastic coverings on the lines, and spliced the wires. Using black mechanical tape, he wrapped the wires and dug a hole in the frozen ground to bury the new splice.

"I sure hope that was the problem," he said, getting to his feet. Back at the battery assembly, the cables reconnected, he saw the spark and heard the motor of the solar array. It rotated, towards the late evening sun dumping off the accumulated snow. If they had power tonight it would be a blessing, but he wasn't sure there was enough sunlight left or enough stores left in the batteries to give them light for the night, which meant he needed to get dinner going.

Putting away his tools, he checked on the well pump, satisfied with his work before heading inside the house. In the kitchen, he turned on the tap and a slow trickle of water began to run.

"Yay!" Johnnie yelled.

"Yeah, big whoop," he replied, trying to give the boy an encouraging smile. His smile faded when he went into the bedroom to change out of his wet clothing and realized the bed had been soaked with snow. "Can I catch a fucking break with this shit?"

Snatching the bed covers off the bed, he dragged the mattress to the kitchen, placing it on the floor by the stove. He added a few more logs, hoping the heat would dry the mattress. Luck seemed to favor him as he opened the second bedroom door and Johnnie's bed, thankfully, had not been under the hole. Johnnie's bed was dry but the room was a mess. A light flickered in the kitchen and the power was coming back on.

"At least there's that," he mumbled, closing the door to keep the heat contained in the living room. Thinking better of it, he opened it up to let the room get warm. At least the boy would have a bed to sleep in tonight.

Cotter's stomach rumbled and he needed food. The stew meat was in the kitchen sink. Moving it to the side, he washed his hands before cleaning the meat and starting the stew. The smell of the browning beef in the pot made Judy's mouth water.

"I'm not even hungry again, but that sure smells good, Mister," Johnnie said.

"Cotter," he told the boy. "My name is Cotter Wihlborg."

"Mr. Wihlborg, I said a prayer today thanking Jesus for Daddy sending you to help us," Johnnie said. "Another man came here looking for Daddy too, but he didn't stay to help. He did say he would be back to get something he was looking for, but I don't know what that is."

Cotter stopped dicing carrots and his eyes went to Judy. Her lips pressed closed together and her eyes teared. Johnnie filled him in on what Judy was unwilling to say in front of the child.

"Mama said he was a bad man, and that if he ever came back that I needed to hide," Johnnie said, picking up a carrot chunk and biting into it.

"If he comes back, I'll be here and ready for him," Cotter said, still looking at Judy. "Did he happen to say what he was looking for, Mrs. Morrow?"

She shook her head no, but her eyes said otherwise. This was no time to play games with him. Cotter squinted his eyes.

"Mrs. Morrow, if you know what he is a looking for or if you have it, I need to know what I am dealing with," Cotter said.

"Honestly, I don't know," she said truthfully. "Caleb owed a lot of people, who sometimes came here looking for him. Usually, we could hear them coming down 440, since there's not a lot of traffic back here, and hide, but that last one knew all of our tricks. He was waiting for us, with a gun."

"Can you describe him?"

"New Jersey thug type, dark hair, scar over his left cheek, beady eyes," she said.

"Hmmpf," was all Cotter added, going back to his task of making the stew. He knew the man and who the man worked for, which meant Caleb had been in more trouble than just running from him. He was also running from some bad men. His thoughts went to the box in his truck. Adding two and two, he came up with four more levels of hatred for Caleb Morrow.

He sent a box of death to his wife and kid. Whatever was inside, bad men wanted it back. Even if she returned what was inside, the men wouldn't let her or the kid live. The lights popped on and in the background a kid's song began to play.

*Ring around the Rosie, a pocket full of posies, one, two three, we all fall down.*

It was an omen. She needed to get on her feet and fast. He'd sent The Company confirmation of job completion. Word would soon spread that Caleb was dead. If she had an insurance policy on the dunderhead, those men would want it and the box. *Damn you, Caleb. Damn you to an eternal hell.*

Judy saw the look on his face and understood that this man knew. He didn't know all of it, but as soon as she got on her feet, she needed to tell him the truth. An ugly truth that she still had yet to face herself.

# Chapter Three – Moving & Shaking

In the wee hours of the morning, as the blackness of night touched the arrival of the awakening morning, Princess Morgan tiptoed into her daughter's bedroom, sitting on the side of her bed. Gentle hands shook the child awake as she placed a finger over her daughter's lips to silence the child.

"Ssssh Judy, I need you to get up and get dressed, really quiet okay," Princess said to the 10-year-old girl.

At the tender age of 10, Judy Morgan knew the routine. Her Mama was leaving the current boyfriend, a round-bellied man named Otis, who always asked Judy to sit on his lap when her Mama wasn't home. Having been trained by the best grifter in the land, Princess had taught her daughter the right words to tell her boyfriends should they ever ask to take such a liberty with her.

"I'm too old to sit on your lap," Judy told old Otis.

"You are never too old to sit on your Daddy's lap. Just think of it like talking to Santa," Otis said, giving the girl a tobacco-stained smile.

"I'm too old to believe in Santa and you ain't my Daddy," Judy said, watching his face. She knew the next tactic, one of anger, fear and intimidation.

"Get your little ass over her girl and do as I say, or I will throw you and your Mama out on the street," Otis said with a sneer.

"And if you do then I'll call the police. I'm going to tell them you came in my room last night and put your finger inside of me," she said. "Mama said when men do that, they go to prison, and the other men in prison turn them into their bitch. Mr. Otis, I don't want you to be a man's bitch, so please, just don't touch me, okay?"

He didn't much care for the girl – she was a smart one. His eyes were wide in shock as he stared at the pretty ebony skinned little girl. She was too scrawny for his taste, but in a pinch, a warm tight hole was a warm tight hole.

"Fuck you and your crazy ass Mama," Otis declared, struggling out of his big chair onto the wide, smelly flat feet. "I want both of you out by the time I get home from work tonight. Let you Mama know I said so."

"Tell her yourself," Judy said, watching the man take a step towards her. She held her chin high, almost daring him to strike the angelic face, but he only pushed her by the shoulder out of his way.

They didn't leave that night. It wasn't Princess' way. She needed at least two days to access Otis' bank accounts, clear the contents, and make off with the man's money. Well, that's the way she'd done the last man, Henry. Before that, it was Judy's father, Eugene Morgan, who eventually caught up with them, but his money was gone and Princess was then playing house with Henry.

Henry, she stole his entire wallet, maxed out the credit cards, and reported him for attempted sexual assault on her 8-year-old daughter. Judy didn't like the way Princess did things. Henry had been a nice man. He was the last nice one they lived with as the Foxy Brown, Cleopatra Jones look that Princess was known for began to fade. Her ability to pull the men with good money eroded along with the perky breasts she showcased as conversation starters. However, she made sure they always had a roof over their heads and ate well.

Fast forward to two years later and a bus ride from Portland, Oregon to Denver, Colorado because there was only enough money in Otis' account to get them that far and a fleabag hotel room for two nights. That's how long it usually took Princess to find a new mark. As a lounge singer with a voice of legend, all it took was a walk-on in a pricey casino to sing a few songs, and the men flocked to her. She was smart. Princess never really chose the smart or bright men to give them a good life. Her Mama had a knack for picking the loser, just on the left side of shady, who might want to try a thing or two, or might not. For Judy, she didn't like the way her mother played with her life.

In Denver, a partially blind man named Herbert who enjoyed sucking soup through a straw was her next mark. At 12 years old, Judy truly understood her mother wasn't a good person by the things she did to old Herbert. That ride could have gone on forever, but Herbert's son didn't like Princess. Herbert's son did like a 12-year-old Judy, a bit too much for Princess' liking and again in the middle of the night, they were on the way to New Orleans.

At 14, Judy learned to pick pockets during Mardi Gras and roll drunks in back alleys for money. A jazz musician, aptly named Miles, taught the young woman how to watch out for bad men. He also taught her how to count cards, cook, and actually clean a house. Princess wasn't a whiz in the kitchen. Inappropriately, one morning, Miles explained to a 14-year-old Judy, that, "Man, you mama can't cook worth a damn! I guess that's why she has porn star abilities in the bed."

"You don't need to tell me that," Judy said.

"You're right, I'm sorry," Miles apologized. "I'm curious though, Judy, what do you want to be when you grow up? You gon' be like yo' Mama, or you gonna be better?"

"I'm going to be better," she said. "My child will have a home. A permanent one."

"I see," Miles said, saying no more.

She liked Miles. He was a stand-up guy. One of the last semi-decent ones, but Princess, being herself, became jealous of his relationship with Judy. Although several times Judy tried to explain to her mother that he treated her like a daughter, Princess didn't want to hear it.

"Your fucking father didn't treat you like a daughter," Princess said. "You never trust men, Judy! Never. They get close to use you. Once you are used up, they discard you like trash. It's best to get them before they get you."

She was 16 when they arrived at the bus station in Atlanta, a bustling town filled with movers and shakers and well-dressed Black people. She had never seen so many affluent African Americans in her life who drove nice cars, had nice homes, and went to work every day to jobs at offices in tall buildings. Gerald, her mother's latest mark, had one of those jobs and two cars. Princess didn't drive and the Atlanta traffic was too much for the woman. She wouldn't allow Gerald to teach Judy to drive either.

The life with Gerald ended when Princess came home early and found him in bed with another man. He asked her to join them in the party, which sent Princess into a rage. The police came at Gerald's insistence because Princess was attempting to castrate him.

Judy never wanted to leave Atlanta, but thanks to Gerald's connections, and Princess' insistence on going to the media to out his down low lifestyle, he set her up with a sweet gig in Chicago. The gig even came with her own apartment. However, it didn't take Princess long to hook up with Clem, who had bad news written all over him.

"Mama, there's something wrong with that man," Judy said. "His eyes aren't right. The thinking is wrong. That man freaks me out."

"Child, ain't I taught you nothing?" Princess asked.

"Yes, you taught me to follow my instincts and never trust a man," Judy said. "I'm telling you I don't trust him. We have a good thing. You're paying your own rent, making a decent wage. This is the one time we don't need a man to survive."

"Baby, it's about more than just surviving," Princess said. "In the middle of the night, when it's just you and your man, there is a sweet spot of connection that you'll understand one day."

The day didn't come. At 18 years old, Judy came home to find her mother dead, a deep red gash from one ear to the other, displaying Princess's throat being cut from one end to another. Her mother's wallet was gone and the bank account empty. Luckily for them both, her mother's account was butter and egg money. The main account was in Judy's name as an insurance policy. It wasn't the only policy Judy kept. Using money from her part-time job, she had taken out a life insurance policy on Princess, paying $10 a month to ensure that when the time came, life wouldn't leave her as Cinderella's work shoes. The apartment would be missed, but Clem would not.

Clem was nowhere to be found, but sticking to what her mother taught, she took only the small tokens of their life in Chicago. Princess's nice jewelry pieces that would get pawned in lean times went in her backpack. A photo of she and her mother as well as one of Judy and Miles were the only items that were of personal value to her. The apartment meant nothing. Although it had been their only permanent home since she was 10, whoever killed her mother could come back to get her. She wasn't waiting for that to happen.

Saying farewell to her mother with a modest cremation service, she loaded her one suitcase and took a bus to New York. Before she left, she notified the insurance company of the passing of her mother and her forwarding PO Box in Brooklyn at a UPS Store. The nice boss at her part-time job put in a reference for Judy in New York, saying she was good worker ensuring the young woman had a job when she got to Brooklyn.

For three years, she worked her ass off, saving as much as she could in the rainy-day account and put in for a transfer to Atlantic City where she met Robert, a cute young man with no real ambition other than to be a rapper.

She asked one night as she lay close to him, "What about a home? A family? A yard for the dog and kids to run in with fresh air?"

"Naw, that ain't the life for me. I'm a city boy. I'm an action junkie," Robert told her.

She appreciated his honesty, but it wasn't what she wanted in life. For too long, she'd had nothing and the last thing she needed was a man who wanted short term gains and flashing lights. Princess lived under flashing lights on stage, creating an illusion of a woman going places who moved often, but never got anywhere. It wouldn't be Judy's life.

There were no buses in the walking away from Robert, just a nice note that read, "We want different things." She would miss the nights the sweet spot of connection her mother had talked about. But a girl couldn't eat connection, although Robert did a helluva job eating the sweet spot. She deserved more and she would get it.

At the age of 23, Atlantic City had been good to her. Using the card counting trick taught to her by Miles, she made a small fortune, squirreling it away like a chipmunk in winter. Her new boss said he was heading to Vegas to manage a new casino.

"I could use a sharp cookie like you, Judy," he told her. "I need a man on the inside that I can trust, and you are just the man for the job."

"Will you provide room and board, plus an airline ticket to Las Vegas?"

"Sure doll," Jimmy the Flint told her.

Two weeks later, she was on her way to Las Vegas, working at a casino in the Freemont experience. This is where she met one Caleb Morrow, a man with a vision. The sweet spot at night consisted of watching DIY television of people living off the grid.

"We could get us a nice piece of land in Missouri, raise some crops, get a living roof, and some solar panels allowing the sun to provide all the power we could ever need," Caleb told her.

Initially she thought he was lying, but on her first vacation, an actual vacation where there were plans to go on a trip and come home, he took her to Missouri. A little plot of land he'd said, turned out to be 20 acres of the most beautiful corner of America she'd ever seen in her life. In a rented Winnebago, parked next to Moniteau Creek, she consented to be his wife. Two years later, as new parents, living in a home they had slaved over and built themselves, she gave birth to their child, Johnnie, a sweet kid who rarely cried and made a doting Momma smile.

Life was good but money was low. Raising crops yielded year-round food, but Caleb wasn't a hunter, which meant no meat. He bought a second used car that needed a fuel pump and an alternator, which he promised to work on and teach her to drive. The same broken-down car sat in the front yard by the broken-down fence a year later.

"Judy, I got a call from Jimmy the Flint," Caleb said one night. Johnnie was four at the time. "He's got some work he needs me to do."

"Caleb, you know Jimmy. That's why they call him the Flint. He's sharp but is good at starting fires," she stated firmly. "We have a good life here. If you go to Jimmy, you won't come back the same if you get back at all. Get a job in town."

But Caleb wasn't a nine to five kind of man. In her heart she knew it was only a matter of time, which is why she never told him about the bank account which she saved for a rainy day. It was nearly $75,000 strong when he left that cold October morning. A year later he hadn't returned. The insurance policy she'd taken out on him had a double indemnity clause. If he died by accidental death, the payout would be grand and she would have enough to put Johnnie through college. She waved goodbye to him on a Monday morning as he took the working car, his old suitcase and the smile which had gotten her into his bed. Promising to call later in the week, she didn't look back as he drove out the yard.

Although he called each Sunday, his voice seemed strained. One Sunday, she heard a woman's voice in the background, and Judy knew her husband wasn't coming home. Never one to be religious, she wasn't going to take up with another man, being married to one already. She did the next best thing – made a call to Jimmy the Flint.

"Accidents usually run around 50,000," he told.

"I wonder if it can be a remote location, where the accident takes a while to allow the blood to run out of his lying heart," she said as twirled a lock of her hair.

"I'll send you a number," Jimmy said, clicking off the line.

No matter how hard she tried to not be her mother, it seemed that every two years she needed to move. Only now, her lungs filled with fluid, her child nearly starved, and no way to leave the house, money in the bank meant nothing to a woman with no internet and no phone. Uncertain if her husband was alive or dead, her soul ached from the pain of failing, to give Johnnie better than she had and a man in the child's life to love and guide the wee sprout into adulthood so her baby wouldn't become the line of faces from her childhood who shared a bed in order to have a roof over its head.

She and Johnnie hid from the men who came looking for Caleb. More than likely, he'd taken something from them and they wanted it back. Unbeknownst to her, the slimeball had taken money from her as well. The secret account wasn't so secret. The remaining twenty-five grand in the account, he'd accessed and siphoned off, leaving she and Johnnie with nothing. With no proof of his death, she couldn't get the insurance money.

The stupid car in the front yard Caleb never fixed for her to even practice at driving, and the town of Rocheport was a good 25 miles away. She couldn't make it in winter with a small child. As much as she wanted to pray for help, it would have been hypocritical to do so, all things considered. Instead, Caleb sent help to them.

Cotter was handsome man, who didn't say much, but worked hard to make sure they ate and she got better. Each day she was stronger, and today, she was on her feet. Weak. Coughing. Still a bit feverish but she was up. Moving would give her strength that she would need to make life go forward. She'd made coffee for them and oatmeal for breakfast, sitting across the table from the man, wrapped in his blanket as Johnnie enjoyed 30 minutes of morning cartoons.

"I never left because this is our home, plus I can't drive, and Caleb took all my money," she confessed.

"Gathered as much," Cotter said, listening to the wet cough. Urging her back to the couch after breakfast with a cup of hot tea, he asked her permission to take Johnnie to town to get a coat and decent pair of boots. She knew pedophiles and men with dark hearts. Cotter didn't have one, but Johnnie had been taught, just as Princess had taught her, to say the right things to stay safe. She let him leave with the child. Trust was all she had. A gnawing feeling inside of her said Cotter wouldn't leave her here to die.

When the man returned, he also brought with him a fold-a-way bed to sleep on in the living room. It seemed he planned to stay awhile. There was a darkness around his soul that stood out like an aura of death attached to him. At this point, if he were Death himself, Judy didn't care. She preferred the Devil who was nursing her back to health versus the one who was going to come calling again, looking for whatever Caleb took.

Life was hard. It was tougher if you were a dumb thief. Her husband was the dumbest of the lot. Yet, she was grateful to him for sending help. Maybe, he hadn't been so stupid after all.

# Chapter Four – Well, I'll Be Damned

Johnnie sat in the backseat of the truck, strapped in and gazing out the window as if they'd just driven into Disneyland. Since the woman didn't drive and Caleb had been gone a while, it was obvious the child hadn't left the homestead. It tugged at the aortic strings around his hardened heart that a sweet kid could get such a rotten deal. The mom didn't seem so bad, but she married a man like Caleb Morrow. In his estimation, that meant she wasn't that good either.

"Hey kid, when was the last time you've seen your old man?" Cotter asked, looking in the rear-view mirror.

"It's been a while," Johnnie said. "I think it was at my birthday. Momma made me a cake with four candles on it. Daddy was home then. Haven't seen him since."

"You miss your old man?"

"Not really," Johnnie said. "Mama says you can't miss what you never really had. She was talking about meat, but I know she meant Daddy."

Cotter looked again in the rear-view mirror at the boy. Scrawny. However, the eyes held a spark and the kid was no dummy. He seemed to pick up on everything said and unsaid. It amused him that the child knew just what to say when asked a question. Never giving away too much, but telling him just what he wanted to know.

"I don't know what size you are, so I hope you don't mind us going to the second-hand store to get you some clothes," Cotter said. "The way you're eating, I can see you tripling in size in no time."

"Second hand? You mean like used clothes?" Johnnie asked.

"Yeah, is that a problem?"

"No, Mama always went to the Goodwill when Daddy took us to town to shop," Johnnie said. "She never bought used underwear though. Or used shoes. Said she didn't want me getting a foot rash from somebody else's dirty toes."

"Smart," Cotter said.

"Yeah, Mama is really smart. She taught me to read, write my name, and do math too."

"You don't go to school?"

"I just turned six," Johnnie said. "I think she said in the fall, I would start first grade. She's been working with me to make sure I won't be behind the other kids when I do. The car should be fixed by then, so she can drive me to the bus stop."

"Good to know," Cotter said, slowing his speed as he drove through Rocheport, connecting to Highway Bb, and then the interstate.

"Where are we going?" Johnnie asked, looking out the window.

"Columbia, they have more stores," Cotter said. "I need to get a few more things that are cheaper in a bigger town."

"If I had some money, I would get Mama something pretty to make her feel better," Johnnie said pausing. "Mister, can I have a few dollars to get her a present. I will work hard to pay you back."

"I tell you what, Johnnie, I will give you $10 and we will call it an allowance," Cotter said, "for all the help you've given me with your Mama and the house."

"An allowance? Cool!" Johnnie said pleased. "Do I get that every week or every month? I have to know so I can make a budget."

Cotter burst into laughter. The kid was growing on him. A bit too much for his comfort, but in every life, there needed to be hope. If there was nothing else, he could give him or his mother before it left, it would be hope. At this point, most of what he offered was a blind hope, because he couldn't for the life of him see it going anywhere, but he was here. So, were they, in the pile of poo together – for now, anyway? In a week or two the woman would be well and he'd be gone on his way. A great deal needed to be done before he left, and staying busy was always a plus.

THE GPS GUIDED HIM to the Salvation Army Family Store where the first item he looked for was a heavy winter coat. Finding one he liked, that had a zip out lining, it wasn't very pleasing to Johnnie who didn't like the color. The kid wanted one in bright orange that looked more like a hunting jacket.

"You sure that's the one you want?" Cotter asked in disbelief.

"I like how bright it is," Johnnie said, locating a pair of matching neon orange socks with the price tag still attached. "Mister Cotter, this pair is new. Nobody's toes have been in these."

He frowned as a saleswoman came over to offer them help. Cotter went down a list of sweaters, long sleeve shirts, and pants that was needed for the growing kid. Since he didn't know the kid's size, the lady offered him assistance.

"I need one for show and one to grow," he said, echoing the words of his mother when she would shop for him as boy. It didn't matter how big the size of a shirt she bought, in less than two months, Cotter seemed to outgrow the material. Johnnie looked as if he would do the same.

Four pairs of jeans, two pairs of pants, and a shirt, which looked more like a salmon colored blouse lay in the cart. A brand-new pair of snow boots, minus a previous pair of owner's feet, were added to the buggy, along with two sweaters, a Kermit the Frog sweatshirt, and four long sleeve shirts. Satisfied, Johnnie, in the neon orange socks, matching coat, and new boots, climbed into the back seat, happy as a lark.

"I'm hungry," the kid said.

"Kinda figured," Cotter replied. "Whaddaya want to eat?"

"Don't know," Johnnie said. "Am I buying my food out of my allowance or is it your treat?"

Cotter laughed again. He was really starting to like the kid a great deal. He drove the two of them to Wal-Mart, which had a Burger King inside. To his surprise, Johnnie didn't want french fries but opted instead for apple slices. He inquired as to why.

"Those fries taste funny," Johnnie offered. "My Mama makes the best fries from real potatoes. Those don't taste real. The chicken nuggets are good though."

"Leave it to me to get stuck with a kid with a refined palate," Cotter mumbled as they ate in silence. Johnnie's eyes followed the young girls with their mothers, taking note of the clothing they wore and hairstyles.

"What are we getting in here, Mister Cotter?"

"Undies, soap, washing powder, that kind of stuff," Cotter said.

"Good, I need a new toothbrush," Johnnie said. "Mine looks like a cartoon character with bad hair."

Cotter found himself laughing again. Bright. Imaginative. The kid had a good imagination even after nearly freezing to death in that hovel of a hand-made house. His hand went to his chest to stop the rush of feeling around his heart.

"You okay, Mister Cotter?"

"Yep. Let's get moving so we can get back and check on your Mama," Cotter said, throwing away their trash.

Johnnie walked alongside him in the neon coat and new snow boots that the kid insisted on putting on in the truck, and they went into the health and beauty section. Toothpaste, new brushes, and soap were added to the basket. The one aisle men never went down made Cotter stop. *She said she'd run out of everything. That means this stuff too.* He thought back to Andrea, his on again off again crazy lover, and the items he'd seen under her bathroom sink. Searching his memory, he reached for the blue package along with a blue box of girly inserts.

"Not those," Johnnie said, reaching up on the shelf to get another brand and different size. "These."

"Thanks," Cotter said, anxious to get out of the aisle, but Johnnie went down another to get lavender soaking salts and a bath sponge.

"My Mama likes these," he said, checking the price and doing the math with his fingers. "Together, these are only $3, which leaves me $7 more to spend. I want to get her a new pair of slippers to keep her feet warm."

"Do you know the size?"

"I think a seven," Johnnie said. "Her feet aren't very big."

"Then let's head to the shoe section," Cotter said.

Johnnie picked a pair of soft lined slippers for $5 for the woman and asked if Cotter could afford a pair for him as well. The pair Johnnie chose were a bright red, making the man wonder if something was wrong with boy as they traveled to the underwear section. Cotter reached for boxer briefs and Johnnie started to laugh really loud in the store.

"What's wrong, you don't like this kind?" Cotter asked.

"They're okay," the kid said with a smile. "But I wear this kind."

The small fingers pointed at a shelf on the opposite side to girl's underwear. Cotter was confused by the expression on his face, which made Johnnie laugh even louder. He took it back, he didn't like the kid. Something was wrong with it and he needed to take it back to its Mama.

"Mister Cotter, I wear panties because I'm a girl," Johnnie said, her face bright with amusement.

"Well, I'll be damned," Cotter said, looking at Johnnie in a whole new light. "Well, shit, I guess we need to go back and get hair barrettes and ribbons too."

"Oooh, can we? Can we?" Johnnie said, clapping together her hands in the new pair of gloves they also scored at the second-hand store.

It was at that moment that Cotter Wihlborg knew he was in trouble. The little imp had fooled him, but moreover, she'd snuck one in on him and impressed the hell out of a man who rarely, if ever was duped. The idea of barrettes in the wild hair brought a smile to his face as he threw a cute pink hat in the basket before heading back to get ribbons for Johnnie's hair.

JUDY FIDGETED ON THE couch, waiting for them to come back. Fear held onto her chest, almost preventing her from breathing at the thought of the man taking her child and not coming back. She didn't know why she trusted him, but she did. Johnnie was smart and she'd taught her child well. However, there was going to come a moment when the man found out that the kid, he'd been calling son was in fact a girl. For safety, living in a remote area, she dressed the child as a boy. Lost people infrequently found their way to the door of the home, and the last thing she needed was to fight off a weirdo who had a thing for young girls. It was bad enough she had to worry about fighting one off that wanted to take liberties with her, let alone her child. The concern eased as she heard the sound of his truck coming up the long drive, bringing her child home safely.

The darkness which surrounded Cotter didn't give off the vibe that he would hurt a child, and he was all she had right now. At his mercy, the blind hope that Cotter would treat them well kept her calm when she got to her feet, feeling stronger this afternoon. The pills he'd been giving her helped to break the fever, but her recovery was a long journey from being over. Adding a log to the fire, she warmed the room as an exuberant Johnnie burst through the door with bags of loot, anxious to show off the goodies she'd scored.

"Mama! Mama! Look at my new coat," Johnnie said. "Mister Cotter gave me an allowance and I was able to get some things for you too!"

Rummaging through the bag, Johnnie pulled out the slippers, helping her mother put them on her feet. "I got ribbons and barrettes for my hair too!" the child exclaimed while showing off the Kermit sweatshirt, orange socks and other items.

"We got new toothbrushes too, Mama!" Johnnie explained. "We even got you supplies!"

She yanked the personal items out of the bag, leaving Judy's eyes wide. Embarrassment showed on her face as she dropped her eyes, not wanting to make eye contact with Cotter.

"It's cool. I have sisters," he mumbled. "Johnnie, we need to wash that stuff before you wear them."

"Yes sir," she said, heading towards the back of the kitchen.

"Oh, you have a washer and dryer?" he asked, shocked.

"A washer, yes, but the dryer is nature or this fireplace," Judy said, sliding the personal items behind her back. "Thank you for all of this. I don't know how I am ever going to repay you."

"We can start by you trusting and being honest with me," Cotter said. "You could have told me the child was a girl."

"I am trusting and being honest with you," Judy said. "I let you take her with me having no phone to call for help and being laid up here with pneumonia."

"It's not pneumonia," he said. "You are just really sick and need nutrition and hydration. Yeah, the lungs are wet with sputum, but not to the point of all of that. Speaking of no phone..."

He tossed an unopened prepaid phone towards her. "This way, you have a phone. Later, I'll program in my number."

"Are you leaving?" she asked, suddenly aware of not wanting the man to leave them alone. The idea of his presence not filling the space evoked fear inside of her soul. The last thing she needed or ever wanted was to rely on a man, but this one she needed.

"Not yet," he said.

The look of relief on her face touched him. It had been a long time since a woman wanted him to stay around. Even longer since he'd found one, he wanted to be around for longer than a few nights. Touching her hand, he went to check on the meat he left simmering in a Dutch oven on the stove.

"Cotter?" she said softly.

"Yeah Mrs. Morrow?"

"Judy. Call me Judy and it doesn't matter," she said softly.

He turned his head, looking over his shoulder at her. The soft glow from the fireplace lit her face, giving him the first real look at the woman. Even sick, she was kinda pretty.

"What doesn't matter, Judy?" he said, placing the lid on the pot and reaching for two sweet potatoes.

"Whatever you did. Whatever awful thing you did which makes you feel as if you have to do penance here with us," she said softly. "It doesn't matter. Your willingness to stay and help is all that does."

"I'm not doing penance for any damned thing," he said. "Caleb was..."

Cotter lowered his voice, not wanting Johnnie to hear him say a bad thing about her father. He also needed a minute to phrase his wording just so without giving away clues of how he'd come across Caleb Morrow.

"My husband was many things, but he loved us," Judy lied.

"The only person Caleb loved was himself. He sent me in a last-ditch effort to not rot in hell for leaving the two of you here defenseless," he said. "I have a mother, a brother and sisters. I wouldn't want this for them and would put a bullet in any man who considered this to be a life. Everything we do in this world matters. If not to us, then those it impacts. Caleb's bad decisions impacted that sweet child. He will not continue to hurt either of you."

That's when she cried. He came to her side in six long strides, scooping her up to sit on his lap. The sour scent of sickness, sweat and an unwashed body filled his nostrils, and tonight they both would put their bodies in some water. He actually needed a hot shower as well and looked forward to washing off two days of sweat and grime. Holding her to his chest, he didn't rock or offer words of consolation, just the strong arms of protection in her time of need.

Judy actually let go and cried the tears of hatred, fear, and frustration she'd held onto for so many years. Cotter was a bad man too. In her soul she knew it. Miles. Henry. The whole lot of men who straddled the line of good and bad were all bound up in this one body who sat still, cradling her in strong arms, holding her as she cried.

More tears came as she cried for herself, feeling some sort of way at being held by this man. The warmth of his touch. The tenderness of his care. She wanted more than anything to be well so she could repay him by sharing the sweet spot of connection in the middle of the night between a man and a woman. It was all she had to give him.

Judy hoped it would be enough for now.

# Chapter Five- What Next...Damnit!

The oddity of the feelings engulfing him made Cotter want to pack his overnight bag and get the hell out of the house. As the three of them sat around the table eating dinner, the conversation, totally monopolized by Johnnie, reminded him of the days when his father would come home off the road. Cotter would fill the table with every detail that Boubacar Wihlborg missed in his absence while making money for his family. His sisters, Alayna and Susie would get in a word every now and then, but while his father was away, Cotter was the man of the house. He had to fill his Pops in on man details and how he kept the house safe.

*Footsteps.*

*Outside of the backdoor.*

*Crunching on the snow.*

Cotter held up his hands, pointing at the two womenfolk, asking them to get down under the table as he went for his bag and retrieved the 9mm gun. Walking softly, he made his way towards the back door, cutting the kitchen lights and crouching under the window. Giving his eyes time to adjust, he raised his head to peer out the window and spotted a man. Yanking the door open, he pointed the gun at the man's head, who was very surprised to see him.

"What the fuck you doing here?" Cotter asked.

"Shhherrrrifffff," the man stuttered.

Cotter reached behind the door and flipped on the light to see the Sheriff's uniform and lowered his weapon. Grabbing the doorknob, he walked out and pulled the door closed behind him and put his weapon in the waistband of his pants. He eyeballed the Sheriff with suspicion.

"Why are you sneaking around at the back door instead of coming to the front and where's your vehicle?" Cotter asked.

"It's about a mile down the road," the Sheriff replied. "I saw a couple of vehicles come this way and one was, I guess, your truck. Didn't know anyone was still here. Just wanted to peek in before I knocked and got my fool head shot off."

"Sheriff, you still nearly got your fool head shot off," Cotter said, not wanting to invite the man inside, but he knew the Sheriff's type. He would continue to come back again and again until he got to see inside. Allowing the timber of his voice to rise enough for Judy and the kid to hear him he asked, "You wanna come in for coffee? It's a cold night."

"A cup of coffee would be really good right now," the Sheriff said.

"Come on in," Cotter offered.

JUDY AND JOHNNIE CROUCHED under the table, listening to Cotter talk to the Sheriff. It had been a few months since the sheriff had been out to the place, and each time he'd come, Caleb wasn't anywhere to be found. Each time he'd conveniently dropped by with one excuse or another, she only referred to Caleb as 'my husband', never giving his actual name. Whispering in Johnnie's ear, she provided the child instructions on what to do when the Sheriff came inside the house.

"You understand, Johnnie?" she asked, clinging to the child.

"Yes, Mama," Johnnie replied as the sound of the back door opened, bringing in a brisk of cold air, Sheriff Rottingham, and the man she was going to call her own. At least for tonight.

Climbing from under the table, Judy quickly cleared the dishes and grabbed two cups for coffee. Using a couple of Johnnie's new barrettes, she quickly smoothed down her hair, clamping away the wayward strands. She didn't have any dessert to offer, leaving the coffee to be just enough to get the man in and out of the house. A phony smile plastered itself on her face as the men came inside from the cold.

"DADDY!" JOHNNIE CRIED out, running to Cotter and flinging her small body at him. He lifted the girl into his arms, holding her close to his chest.

"It's okay, sweetie, it's just the Sheriff. There's no need to be frightened," he said in his best, put on Daddy voice. "Honey, let's get the man some coffee to warm him. It's cold out there tonight."

"Sure thing," Judy said, pretending to feel better than she did. "Sheriff, you want milk and sugar with that coffee?"

"No ma'am, black and strong is how I like it," Sheriff Rottingham said, cutting his eye at the woman.

"My Judy knows I take mine the same way," Cotter said. "Nothing like a good, strong, black cup of anything to make a man anxious to get home and protect what's his."

"You travel a lot there, Mister...?"

"Wihlborg," Cotter said. "Cotter Wihlborg. Used to drive over the road for a while, then took a bit of contract work, but all that is behind me. I'm home to stay."

The Sheriff took a swig of the coffee, asking a few more questions as Johnnie sat in Cotter's lap, looking with one eye at the Sheriff as if he would harm her "new Daddy." Judy sat across the table, giving Cotter a look of love and admiration that warmed him all the way to his toes. She clung to his every word as if he were Moses sent to deliver the Commandments to the Hebrews, thirsty from wandering about the desert.

"Sorry, I don't have any dessert to offer you, Sheriff, but I can make you a chicken sandwich to take with you," Judy said.

"Naw, coffee is just enough," the beady-eyed man said, getting to his feet. "I hope that gun of yours is registered."

"All my weapons are registered," Cotter offered him with a smile. "I was wondering though, since this is my land, can I hunt on it all year? I mean, when the game is in season."

"Yeah, you can, but we don't have much in the way of processing places, other than ole Jeb, who is blind in one eye and got a cataract in the other," the Sheriff said.

"No need for all that," Cotter said. "I can field dress anything and barely leave a trace of blood."

It was the way he said which made the Sheriff shiver. "Cotter Wihlborg, you said?"

"Yep, Wihlborg," he replied, spelling it out for the man. "W-i-h-l-b-o-r-g."

"Nice to see you, Judy, Johnnie," the Sheriff said, headed for the front door. "Sorry to interrupt your meal and scare the little one."

"It's quite alright. It's time for a bath, story time, and bed anyway," Cotter said.

Johnnie was still in his arms as he escorted the Sheriff out the front door, offering him a ride back to his vehicle. The Sheriff stopped on the front porch, looking about the snow-covered yard. It was good land. Land he'd wanted for himself.

"Is Johnnie in school?"

Cotter was grateful for the information shared earlier by the kid. "In the fall. Johnnie just turned six a little while ago. Judy's working really hard teaching her math, reading, and how to write in print and such, so the munchkin won't be behind when school starts."

"Good to know," the Sheriff said, touching the brim of his hat and walking out in the dark of night.

Cotter put Johnnie on her feet, gently pushing her away from the door as he watched the Sheriff's body disappear into the wood line. The man made him uneasy. He'd come to check on the woman. His words, double-edged, were a warning and Cotter fired back with subtlety. A sense of pride filled him at Judy and the kid's quick thinking. The Daddy thing was a nice touch. It felt real to him and to the Sheriff's eyes, but trust was hard won in Cotter's. That man was up to something. Closing the door slowly, he could hear the wood hitting the burning logs in the fireplace as Johnnie added a log to cut the chill.

Securing the door, he faced his new family, watching their faces. "Nice touches," he said.

"That man is a menace," Judy said. "He sneaks about the place often, looking in, checking, for what I'm not sure."

"It's not very late, but does he come by often?"

"At least every other month," Judy said.

"How many times has he met Caleb?"

"He's never met him, and I only gave him my maiden name, Morgan," she said.

"Smart. Really smart," Cotter said, smiling at Johnnie. "That Daddy thing was a nice move."

"I don't know what all Caleb was involved with and with whom," she told him. "The less people know the better. I see you gave him your name and the spelling."

"The best way to lie is to tell the truth," Cotter said. "He's going to check me out."

"Those things you said, contract, over the road driver, those things were true?"

"Are true," he corrected, looking about for his bag. "I need a shower. Does the water get really hot?"

"Shower's broken," Johnnie said. "The tub also leaks water on the floor. Me and Mama usually wash off in the sink, but we hadn't been able to do that in a while, you know, frozen well and all. I sure would love a bath and to wash my hair and put in those really pretty barrettes."

Johnnie eyeballed Cotter when she said the words and he frowned. A hot shower sounded amazing, but now he couldn't have one. He was too much of a man to wash off in a sink and needed an alternative. Two of the three large water bottles sat in the kitchen. The kid would only need half of one to get the crud off her tiny body. Judy maybe the other half. He was going to need a whole one.

"What next...damnit?" he exclaimed, looking at them both. An idea struck him and he planned to go with it. Smiling as he set his idea into motion, Judy and Johnnie watched the man go to work. As understanding dawned, they too began to smile at his idea.

# Chapter Six – Cleaning Up

Cotter filled every large pot he could load onto the cookstove with water from the tap. Extra logs of wood were added to the hopper to make the oven heat quickly to warm the water and the room. The pitcher, which he imagined in the summer to be filled with slices of lemons and just enough sugar for a great lemonade, he also filled with water, taking it out the backdoor. Judy and Johnnie listened as he flipped over the old wash tub, pouring in the pitcher of water, sloshing it about quickly, before dumping the contents on the ground. The water pooled in the recess of snow, where the Sheriff's footprint was indented, quickly freezing solid.

"Shit, it's cold out here!" Cotter mumbled, dragging the tub inside the house and slamming the door shut. The same tub he'd used to house the meat until the power resumed to the house would serve as a great tub in which to wash their bodies. Leaning the metal against the grate of the fireplace, he stood, briskly rubbing his arms to warm his hands.

"Ooh, I need to get my towel and some soap," Johnnie said, running to the bathroom.

"Bring the shampoo and your comb too, Johnnie," Judy called out, falling into a coughing spell, hocking up a wad of phlegm that she spit into a tissue and threw into the fireplace.

"Will you be able to wash her hair?"

"The show we put on for the Sheriff took a bit out of me, so you're going to have to do it," she said to Cotter.

"The hell you say!" He said aloud, his cheeks warming.

The expression on his face was priceless, forcing a surprising amount of laughter from the lungs still filled with sputum, which made Judy cough. As the sputter of coughing ended, the smile stayed. A smile which reached out to Cotter, caressing his face with a softness that needed no physical touch. He felt it. High and low.

"It won't be difficult, I'll walk you through it," Judy offered.

Grumbling, scowling, and reaching for the extra blanket he'd used to wrap Judy's body in for extra warmth, he laid it on the floor. The tub, no longer frigid cold, he placed on the blanket as a happy Johnny stood close by with a towel, soap, and her pajamas ready to climb in. Cotter, using oven mitts, carried the first large pot of water to the tub, pouring it in. Steam rose from the connection between cold metal and hot water. Carrying the pot back to the sink, he refilled it with water from the tap, putting it back on the stove to heat for the Mom's bath to follow. Hefting the five-gallon water bottle onto his shoulder, he carried it to the tub, pouring in half the contents. Cotter bent over, his fingers testing the water.

"One more pot of hot water and it will be just perfect," he said as he moved back to the stove. He loaded the tub with another pot of hot water, bent, tested it and nodded to Johnnie that it was the perfect temp for her bath. "Climb in, kiddo."

His phone rang, and he looked down at the number. It was a call from his boss at The Company. Cotter excused himself from the room as a bare-chested six-year-old happily climbed inside the tub, splashing in the water. He knew later, after they'd gone to bed, he would feel the same damned way at a chance to get clean.

"Stop," he said into the line, using his contracted license name with the organization in which he worked for nearly 10 years. It was a stupid name, but as an ongoing joke between him and the other contracted agents, his reputation of the buck stopping with him, it took hold and stuck. His assigned name was thereinafter, Stop. Beauty loved calling Cotter that name, at least until Caleb Morrow ruined his stats for the past year.

"Proof of contract fulfillment has arrived, and payment will be sent in the morning," Beauty Kurtzwilde said to him. "Are you ready to get back to work?"

"No, not yet," Cotter said.

"A year is a long time to go without an assignment," she said softly, "unless of course you are moonlighting on the side."

"Nope," he said back, thinking of all the alone time he had in the past year to contemplate his existence. Chasing a man across a continent tended to make one rethink how, in fact, they were living their lives. For him, it was barely living at all. He wasn't sure if he wanted to go back to the easy money of erasing problems for people with too much disposable income. A looming fear was that at one point, he would become a problem that an angry wife, cousin, or sister would want handled. Moonlighting was the last thing he wanted to do.

"Good, because that would be a breach of contract between us and you how I feel about disloyal men," Beauty said.

"Give me a month or two to get situated and I'll call in when I'm ready," Cotter said, listening at the door for Johnnie's call to wash her hair.

"Stop, you matter to us at The Company. You also matter to me," Beauty said.

For Cotter, the ones who mattered most to him were in the other room. A little girl in need of having her hair washed and a sick woman in need of a bath. It had been a long time since he'd been needed. They needed him, and he wouldn't leave the ladies to fend for themselves in a world ready to devour them whole.

"Sounds good. I'll await your call," Beauty said. "Just don't be too long. A man with your skills shouldn't allow such traits to rust."

Cotter disconnected the call. Caleb Morrow had taken every skill Cotter had to track the asshole down. Each time he got close and zoomed in, the slippery bastard wormed his way out of the trap to make his death look accidental. He was tired of things slipping between his fingers.

"Mister Cotter! Mister Cotter! The water is getting cold, and I'm ready for my hair to be washed!" Johnnie called from the living room.

He slipped the phone into his pocket as he opened the bedroom door. Judy waited on the couch, watching her little girl, happy in the tub of water. Such a small thing meant so much to a child who'd experienced too little. This house was her choice. Marrying Caleb had been her choice. Johnnie deserved better. She looked up at Cotter coming from the bedroom, the phone slipping into his pocket.

"Hey Johnnie, put your washcloth across your lap please," he asked, but smiled when he saw that it had already been done. "Judy, you may need to walk me through this."

"It's just hair. Wet it, lather the strands, and come through it when it's wet, and rinse once more," she said. "After that, pull it back into a ponytail, braid the loose hair, and then tie it up so it dries overnight."

"Yep, I heard wet it," Cotter said.

Judy threw her head back and laughed, a melodic sound that thumped at the bands around his chest which strapped down his heart. He felt like the Grinch hearing the Whos celebrate Christmas with no gifts.

"I'll walk you through it," Judy said, trying to tamp down the coughing. Step by step she watched as the large hands wash Johnnie's hair, rinse it, and comb through the mass of tangles. It took three tries for his large fingers to figure out the hair bands. The ponytail was crooked, the braid lopsided and uneven, but the look of pride on his face was greater than when he was finished repairing two holes in the roof.

Cotter left the room while Johnnie dressed. During Mommy and daughter story time, he emptied the tub, filling it just enough for Mom to take her bath. Just as the water reached the perfect temperature, he told her the water was ready.

Johnnie was now in bed and sleeping.

"I'll be in the other room," he said softly.

"No, please stay," she said. "I'm going to need your help to wash my hair as well."

"Nope, not a good idea," Cotter said. "You are still in jeopardy and don't need a wet head overnight. Just bathe, and I can help you wash it tomorrow in the sink."

"Okay," she said, sounding disappointed. "Will you at least wash my back?"

"Nope, not a good idea," Cotter said. "I'm still a man. A very heterosexual man, Judy."

"And I haven't been touched by a man in nearly two years," she said. "Cotter, a woman needs to be touched. I need you to touch me."

He exhaled deeply, wanting to turn and walk away from the mess of a conundrum this move would place him in, but he also needed to give the woman what she wanted. It took a few moments for his feet to move his body closer to the sofa, where he took a seat in front of the fire, which rested behind the tub, dancing light off her ebony skin. The small breasts sat high on her chest, the buds hardening under his intense gaze. Small, delicate hands lifted the washcloth, adding soap making the rag sudsy, and then she handed it to him.

"Lord Jesus," he sighed, taking the rag into his fingers. He walked away from her to gather his thoughts. At the sink, he took the pitcher, adding more water from the tap and then hot water from the stove. Tapping the contents with his fingers, he tested it to ensure it wasn't too hot for her skin. His feet felt like lead when he took measured steps back to the tub where she waited patiently for him. Getting to his knees, he observed her closely before doing anything.

Judy's legs were bent in the tub, folding her five-foot-seven frame into a protective position, providing shielding for her breasts as her body faced the fire. In the tub, Johnnie's small body had allowed her to extend her legs, giving the child room to actually sit in the water. Cotter dipped the rag into the pool of water, squeezing the contents onto the smooth skin of her back. With his free hand, he placed it in the center of her back, smoothing over the skin, feeling for warmth where her lungs were located.

"It's still warm, which means there's a lot of fluid still in there, but for two days, you are progressing nicely," he said softly.

She didn't respond as he used the cloth, making small circles on her back, washing her gently. The cloth cleaned the skin all the way to the pool of water which shielded her buttocks from his view. In his left hand, he lifted the pitcher, pouring the warm water over her back, rinsing away the sudsy residue. He didn't know what made him continue, but he reached for her right arm, freeing it from her knees, and began to wash it as well. He did the same for the left arm, moving around the tub, tapping her knee.

Judy lifted her left leg, allowing it to hang over the rim of the tub as he soaped the cloth, then washed her leg. Cotter repeated the action with the right leg, pouring water over the tops of both before moving to her toes. He washed in between each one, with surgical precision, never looking at her face.

"You have nice feet," he said as he lifted the first one over the pool to rinse, followed by the other. Giving the rag to her, he stood. Her eyes raked over his body, searching for signs of interest in what he'd just done. To her disappointment, she found none, and he left the room, closing the bedroom door where he stayed until she was done and dressed.

In the bedroom, he flopped back on the bed, proud of himself. His body throbbed in need now that he was away from the woman. The erection nearly poked a hole in his pants, and he found the urge to rub one out each time he heard the slosh of water, knowing she was washing the good parts and he couldn't see it. To him, it was better this way. His imagination did the work as he stared at the hole in the ceiling he'd covered from the outside. He knew he had to fix the inside as well. Focusing on the other tasks that needed to be completed around the house, the erection ebbed and he felt a little less like a horny wolf ready to gobble up the pig in the straw house.

"Cotter, I'm all done and dressed," she said softly.

"Okay, be right there," he said, sitting up. He, too, was ready for a bath as he got to his feet. He passed her standing at the door, smelling fresh and clean. *Apples. I should have gotten some apples.* The thought of an apple in the little pig's mouth, drizzled in honey made him smile as he dragged the tub to the back door and dumped the contents.

It was his turn for a bath, methodically he added water, hot and cold, to the tub. She'd left a towel and washcloth for him on the couch. This time she lay on the bed, unable to get comfortable at the thought of him, all six feet of hunky out there in that small tub. His legs would hang over the side as he tried to wash all of that body. Judy started to wonder if he had a hairy chest and arms. Maybe hairy legs. She wouldn't know if she stayed in the bedroom.

Listening closely, she heard his zipper come down, then the clunk of his boots as he removed them. Her mind went into overdrive at the idea of him removing the heavy winter shirt, all bare-chested and sitting that tight little bum of his in the water. Unable to stand it any longer, she got to her feet. *He washed my back. I should wash his.*

When she opened the door, his eyes grew wide as he sat in the tub. The long legs hanging over the side had just enough hair on them, but not too much. Scars and bruises covered his torso and she dropped her eyes as she went to the stove. He'd used all the hot water in the pots, so she made a fresh one, waiting with her back to him as it warmed. Giving it just enough time to get the chill off the water, she added it to the pitcher, walking towards him in the tub, all vulnerable at her mercy.

"What are you doing?" he asked with his eyes wide, placing the washcloth over his lap. Even if he bent his knees, the man wasn't going to fit in the tub.

"Returning the favor," she said as she got to her knees. The washcloth she snatched from his hands exposed his floating scrotum in the water. Sticking the cloth in the pool, she soaped the rag, then began washing his back. Just as he'd done for her, she rinsed, and moved to his arms, followed by his legs and his feet.

"You also have nice feet," she said. "Most men who wear boots have yellow toenails and thick layers of dead skin. It seems you take care of yourself."

"I try," he said, watching her face.

She coughed a few times as she worked. Unlike him, she didn't stop at his feet. She moved closer to wash his chest. He sat still as she bathed him like she would Johnnie. Her fingers trailed across the scars and what appeared to be old bullet wounds.

"Tell me about these," she said, rinsing the scars.

"Old Army wounds, from Iraq," he said.

"And the phone call? Was that someone waiting for you to come home?" she asked, looking him square in the eyes.

"No, that was my boss, wondering when I was coming back to work," he said truthfully.

"What is it you do for a living, if I might ask," Judy said, dipping the cloth in the water. "I mean, you know how to unfreeze a well, repair a roof, cook, and I'm sure that is only the tip of the iceberg in your skills."

Her hand moved up his thigh, but he grabbed it, stopping her hand from going any further. Not that it would have mattered. His discipline was gone, and the erection poked up in the water like a buoy trying to guide the woman towards danger. All he could think about was that stupid Baby Shark song. Only he was Daddy Shark, and the tune buzzed in his head, doo doo doo doo doo doo.

"My Dad drove over the road which meant he was gone much of the time," Cotter said. "My Mother was a waitress in a diner in Minnesota, so I know about cold weather, wells freezing over and such."

"Was it just you and your Mom?" she asked, standing to retrieve more hot water to pour in the tub.

"No, it was Mom, me, my brother and my two sisters, Susie and Alayna," he said. "Alayna was older by three years and started dating, which pretty much kept her out the house. Susie had trouble making hard boiled eggs, so if I wanted to eat something other than sandwiches, I had to cook. We lost my brother when he was young. So, I taught myself with a few cookbooks from the library."

"Your parents, are they still married?" she asked, pouring the heated water into the tub, after pushing open his knees, exposing the goodies she'd been trying to see.

"No, my Dad created a new family with a woman named Bertha in Detroit," Cotter said. "He left driving over the road, divorced Mom, and moved to Motown. He's still there."

"Tell me about your sisters," she said, playing in the water with the cloth, moving closer to the goodies, pretending to wash the back of his legs.

"Susie is an attorney now," he said. "She is married with two kids, two dogs, and a parakeet with an attitude."

"She sounds like a fun person. And the other, Alayna, is that her name?"

"Yes, she unfortunately, got pregnant by the knucklehead she was dating at 15," he said. "Now she lives with a woman named Katie. The girl she gave birth to, Cicely, was basically left with me most of the time. I kind of raised her. She is in grad school at Northwestern now. Doing well."

He took the rag from her hand, pulling his feet into the tub and standing. The water rippled down his body, over the hairy legs and firm buttocks. He bent, wetting the cloth, talking to her as he washed as if it were something, they did every day.

"Tell me about your family," he said, holding himself and washing his scrotum.

"I'm the only child of a jazz lounge singer named Princess Morgan, who was a grifter that wasn't very good at it," she confessed, getting to her feet to sit on the couch as she watched him wash his private parts. "We moved every two years from city to city until the last man, I think his name was Clem, ended her run. It may have been Clem or one of the many others whose credit cards she stole and ran up or bank accounts she emptied."

"How did you end up with Caleb?" he asked as he rinsed and stepped out of the tub, grabbing the towel and briskly drying himself.

"I met Caleb in Vegas when I worked for Jimmy the Flint," she said, watching his face for name recognition of the old mob head. "Caleb took me on my first real vacation, in a Winnebago. We came here and he showed me this land. 'Here, we will raise our family.' That's what he said and up until two years ago, that's what we did."

"May I ask what went wrong?"

"Caleb was always wrong, and that was the problem," she said. "I wanted desperately to have a place of my own to raise a child and not have to move every few years. Roots. I didn't have any and we were going to plant some here, which is why I didn't leave. The deed to land is in my name. The land is mine and we built this house by hand."

"I can tell," he said, slipping into a clean pair of boxers and flannel lounge pants.

"Teach me to drive," she said, sitting up.

"What?"

"Teach me to drive," she said. "If I know how to drive, we can make it here. Please don't leave us without giving me the skills to survive."

"You need to get well first," Cotter said. "Let's put your energy into that and then we will talk about the rest."

"How long?"

"How long what?" he said, looking down at himself to make sure his shit wasn't still hard as a rock.

"How long will you stay with us? I mean, if no one is waiting for you at home, I am not averse to you...staying," she said, feeling self-conscious.

"Lady, you don't know me," he said.

"What I know is that you came through that door and took care of us," she said. "Even sitting in that water with your dick harder than Greek philosophy, you didn't try anything with me. I can trust you more than I could my jackass of a husband."

"Judy, what happens if ...," he started to say but she was on her feet. Her arms wrapped around his waist and her soft hair pressed against his bare chest.

"No ifs, Cotter Wihlborg," she told him. "If is what got you here. If is why you stayed to help. If can be a nice life for the three of us, if you want it."

The problem with her statement of if-then scenarios was that he did want it. He wanted to watch Johnnie grow up. The idea of driving her to college and unloading his truck with items for her dorm room like he did for Cicely touched him in a way that he hadn't felt in years. *If* had just slapped him upside the head.

# Chapter Seven – A Hunting We Will Go

Judy, sad-faced and slightly disappointed, went to bed alone, understanding Cotter's refusal to join her, but nonetheless unhappy with his decision. His excuse hinged on going hunting in the morning for game and he didn't want to wake her. Offering the used hunting rifle that Caleb had purchased, Cotter refused, stating he had his own. This raised her eyebrows, and he knew she had questions. Before he could or would share her bed, the honor which still rested deep within him whispered the word *truth* into his ear. She needed to know the truth about him before giving herself to man who had killed her husband. To him, he'd done her a favor, but taking a life meant one less lifeline for the remaining journey he had on earth.

In the wee hours of the morning, dressed in warm clothing, he went to his truck. Lifting the back seat where he stored his emergency supplies and work gear, he pulled out his Remington Model 783 Compact Bolt-Action Rifle with scope and silencer. He put four extra bullets in his pocket and headed towards the solar array where he'd initially seen deer tracks. A hearty roast for dinner would be nice and maybe even some deer ribs or chops. The backstrap was always good to put on the grill, which he also found in the back yard. A nice wood-burning grill, made of stone that would get smoking hot for searing meat.

"Where ya going?" Johnnie asked, standing on the back porch in the bright orange coat.

"Hunting. Go back to bed," he said.

"Be careful out there," the child said, blowing him a kiss. Surprising himself, he reached out to grab it and slapped the imaginary affection on his cheek. Johnnie in return took off running from the porch into the snow, flinging her small body at him, providing a hug which tingled all the way to his toes. The hair, still tied down by the scarf Judy had placed on her head, is where he placed an actual kiss, before swatting the child on the back side and pushing the girl into the house.

"That damned kid is wrapping me around her finger," he said softly, watching her close the back door and peer at him through the curtain.

Cotter set off into the wood line. The rifle, cradled across his arms like a child, was his companion as he looked for signs of life. The white ground blanketed in snow crunched under his boots, alerting the game that he was coming for them, making him pause at a vantage point behind a tree to watch the flat land and the early rays of the sun to break. It was colder than snot frozen to an upper lip, which meant the deer would be moving.

"Lord, this a gorgeous land," he mumbled, imagining what it would be like in the spring, all green and lush. He'd seen small signs sticking out of the snow with labels of vegetables indicating this is where her garden grew. Hearing a sound, he crouched down low, taking to one knee while bringing the rifle to rest in the pocket of his shoulder.

A large buck, at least 10 points, came into view. Aiming his rifle, he pointed, inhaled, and squeezed off a round. The buck dropped to the ground. Proud of himself he got to his feet, walking towards the fallen animal, hoping there were hooks on the back porch to hang the prize and dress it.

Crunches in the snow caught his attention as he turned to see a dark figure charging at him. Raising the rifle, he fired a shot, striking the man, who reached him faster than he'd realized. Brandishing a knife, the assailant's arm went up, coming down across his arm, cutting through the jacket and drawing blood.

"Fuck!" Cotter yelled, twisting his body as the man fell to the ground.

The man rolled to his back, but in the dark, Cotter couldn't see his face. He could see the pool of red saturating the snow, and the bullet from the rifle hadn't missed. The man, bleeding, still swung the knife, trying to get Cotter in the leg, but he almost danced as he jumped back.

"Who the fuck are you?" Cotter yelled.

The man, looking up at Cotter, realizing he wasn't in fact Caleb Morrow, asked the same thing, "Who the fuck are you?"

"You're the one trespassing! And you cut me. I should shoot you again!"

"Don't shoot," the man said, groaning. "I'm hit. Bad."

"It's not bad," Cotter said. "I wasn't trying to kill you, just slow you down. Who are you and what do you want?"

"Can you please help me so I don't bleed out in this fucking cold ass snow?"

"Not until you tell me who you are and why you attacked me," Cotter said.

"Thought you were Caleb. That fucker took something that belongs to my boss. Boss wants it back," the man said.

"Well, Caleb is dead, and whatever he took went to the grave with him," Cotter said.

"What? When?"

"A couple of weeks ago," Cotter said. "He sent me to check on his wife and kid. Found them half-starved and freezing. Trying to get some meat to stock the fridge before I go."

"You friends with Caleb?" the man asked as Cotter took to a knee, using a handkerchief to tie around the man's leg.

"That bastard didn't have any friends," Cotter told him, yanking the cloth tight around the wound making the man wince in pain. "I got sisters. Don't take lightly to a woman being defenseless. Just came to help them out."

"Nice of you," the man said. "You fucking her?"

Cotter punched him in the face. He didn't like anyone talking about Judy that way. Especially not this ass wipe.

"I guess that means yes," the man said, scooping up snow and placing it on his lip.

"It means you have no right to speak about the lady that way," Cotter said. "Get your ass up so we can look at that wound and get you on your way."

"You're going to help me?" the man asked, surprised.

"You want me to call the Sheriff and have him come help you?"

"No," he said softly. "Yield. They call me Yield."

Cotter got the man on his feet, bracing his weight on his arm. He knew the name and the brand. A retrieval agent. That's what he did for The Company. It all began to make sense to him now.

"I'm Stop," Cotter said. The tensing of Yield's body meant he knew Cotter's brand as well.

"You on the job?"

"Haven't worked in over a year, thinking of leaving The Company," Cotter said.

"Beauty ain't gonna like it," Yield said, hobbling alongside Cotter to the house. The walk seemed to take forever, but eventually they made it to the back porch.

"I want to leave before she sends Exit to help me transition from the organization," Cotter said. "No one wants to see that fucker coming, if you see him at all. Met him once, and he's a scary dude."

"No kidding," Yield said. "The one who makes my skin crawl is One Way. That man is crazy. He doesn't care how you go, but one way or another, you will be dead."

"Never met him," Cotter said, opening the back door and getting hit in the face with a gush of warm air. The sound brought Judy from the bedroom and Johnnie in jammies, who stared at the man. She turned to run and hide. "It's okay, sweetie, you don't have to hide."

"That's the man!" Judy said bundling her robe around her body. "He's the one that came looking for Caleb and a package! I told him we didn't have anything."

"He knows that now," Cotter said. "I need to get this bullet out and bandage the wound. Do you have a first aid kit?"

"Just the basics, nothing to remove a damned bullet," Judy said, surprised.

"Get me some hot water and a towel while I go to my truck," he said. "Johnnie, help your Mama and see if you ladies can get a pot of coffee on and breakfast started, please."

"Yes sir," Johnnie said, skirting around the scary, scar-faced man.

Cotter bolted out the front door to his truck to secure his emergency kit. The rifle, slung over his shoulder, stayed with him. In the back of the truck in the toolbox, he opened the second compartment, lifting out his first aid box. In it was everything he needed to save a man's life or his own. Antibiotics, coagulants, EpiPens and even a snake bite kit with antivenom, just in case he ever needed it. He was grateful he hadn't used a large bore rifle to hunt with this morning, because if he had, the man would be dead.

Inside the house, Yield sat at the kitchen table, taking note of the unmade bed cot by the fridge and the pajama pants draped across it. In the corner, he spotted The Company issued overnight bag belonging to Stop. *So, he wasn't sleeping with the woman. He was actually here to help them. What's in it for him? He knew of one other agent, Mann, who married a woman and had a life down in Georgia. Men like them didn't get this. Stop was going to make them a family. His family.* A surge of envy coursed through him.

"Let's work on that leg," Cotter said, coming through the door. He paused briefly, taking note of the look on Yield's face. He opened the kit after taking off his jacket, and Judy looked at the contents. Her heart fluttered as she began to add two and two to reach a summation the scar-faced man and the man who was staying in her house had history.

"I can't get a damned break," she mumbled, going to the kitchen to check the coffee and start the oatmeal.

Washing his hands, he donned a pair of plastic gloves and cut away at the fabric to get to the wound. From the kit, he removed a rolled-up piece of leather and handed it to Yield, who nodded and stuck the leather in his mouth. Thinking better of it, he removed it, looking back at Judy then at Cotter.

"You ever met anyone else from the job?" Yield asked while watching Cotter pick up the needle nose tweezers.

"Yeah," Cotter said, focusing on the task at hand. He talked as he worked, shoving the instrument into the bleeding hole, inducing more pain than was necessary. Yield asked the question in front of the woman to let her know that they knew each other and worked together. She needed to know. Now was as good a time as any.

Cotter said, "I worked with Mann in Cali once on a job. I've met Wrong Way, Merge, Falling Rocks, and Hump. It's been a long year."

Yield bit down on the leather, tears rolling from his eyes, his breathing short as Stop dug around in the wound and extracted the bullet. He slumped in the chair while Cotter tended the wound and began to sew it up, after rinsing it out with a saline solution. He knew his co-worker had hurt him on purpose.

"So, Stop," the man said. "When you going back to work? Men like us don't get the happily ever after."

Judy stirred the pot of oats, listening to the ugly hearted scar-faced man try to unseat the few days of joy she'd had with Cotter. Last night had been almost magical, and he respected her, wanted the best for her, and didn't take advantage of her fragile mental state. A lesser man would have taken what he wanted or bedded her the moment her fever broke, but not Cotter.

"Mister Yield, Scar, or whatever the fuck your name is, I know what you are trying to do," Judy said. "You are lucky he'd didn't put that bullet through your heart."

She sat a cup of coffee on the table. "Oatmeal will be ready in a few. I don't have any breakfast meat to offer you, but I can make you a piece of cheese toast," she said, squinting her eyes.

"I appreciate the hospitality, ma'am," he said. "Your meat issue is over. Old Stop here took down a 10 pointer that he needs to get back out there and get before the wolves come a calling."

"You got a deer?" she asked with wide eyes.

"Yep," he said, threading the needle to sew up the man's leg.

"That is awesome!" Judy said, looking at her daughter who hadn't taken her eyes off the scar-faced man. "Johnnie, are you okay?"

"No ma'am. Why is that man here again?"

"He's looking for something he thinks Caleb sent to you," Cotter said. "Did he send you anything in the mail?"

"I haven't checked the mailbox in a month, being sick and all," she said. "It's too far for Johnnie to go by herself. It's at the end of the road."

Cotter closed the wound and got to his feet. He wrapped the stitches in gauze and took his tools to the sink to clean. "I'll go check the mail," he said. "Yield, I don't want any shit out of you or the next bullet won't be in your leg."

Yield held up his hands in surrender. Cotter, putting his jacket on, stomped out the front door, taking his kit along with him. Grumbling, he started the truck and drove to the mailbox. There wasn't much in it other than a few seed catalogs and marketing materials. In the stack, he found one lone letter with no return address scribbled in a man's bold script. Everything in him wanted to hide it, but if this is what Yield was looking for, it would make the man go away. If it was bad news for Judy, he would provide her any comfort he could.

Driving to the house, he'd made up his mind. He planned to stay. There wasn't anything for him in Venture, Georgia other than a two-bedroom house with half-dead plants and a woman who popped in every now and then to give him some halfhearted sex with loud noises. No one needed him there. Here, he was needed.

Dumping the mail on the table, Judy's small hands sorted through the pile. She located the letter and recognized her husband's handwriting. Cotter made himself a bowl of oatmeal as he sat at the table, taking off his jacket, then adding brown sugar to the bowl along with a bit of milk and pat of butter. Judy had set the items on the table with Yield watching her closely as she picked up the envelope, opening it and reading the contents. She said nothing but laid it on the table for both men to see.

"Shit, that's cold," Yield said, reading the letter. No true explanation. No, I love you just that...coldness. The note was simply stated by Caleb that he wasn't coming back and the life of husband and father wasn't for him.

Cotter frowned when he read it, anger rushing through him. The man was an asshole. He wasn't planning to come back when he left. Had he an ounce of decency he could have told her so, instead of having her wait for him, alone in the middle of Nowhere, Missouri with a small child. Stabbing at the oatmeal with his spoon, he took his time, allowing his eyes to go to her face. It held no expression.

"Mister, I hope this provides you with an answer on whatever it was you are looking for, because it obviously isn't here. Caleb is not coming back, he never planned to, and he left nothing for me and his child," she said. "Please finish your meal and be on your way."

"Yes, ma'am," he said. "I may need a ride to my vehicle though. Mr. Stop, can you give me a lift? I can help you load up that deer since it's on the way."

"Thanks," Cotter said, not wanting to eat since he'd lost his appetite. "I appreciate it."

"And I appreciate you not killing me," Yield said, reaching for his coat. "Thanks for the grub and hospitality. I won't bother you again."

Johnnie, who had sat quietly on the couch, came over to Cotter. Pushing at his chest, she forced him to move his seat so she could sit on his lap. Cradling her face against the broad expanse of his chest, he wrapped his arm around the small body, her eyes droopy with the need for sleep.

"Sweetie, go back to bed," Judy urged her daughter.

"She's fine. I'll put her down in a few," Cotter said, kissing the child on top of the head. He let her sleep as hunger urged him to eat the bowl of oatmeal, eaten slowly as Mr. Yield observed the tender moment between the once hardened hitman and a child. *Stop loves the kid. She must remind him of someone from his former life. His own kid?*

THEY DROVE IN THE TRUCK in silence until they reached the deer. Luckily, no animals had come along to gnaw or nibble on it. Cotter used the wench in back of his truck to haul the animal into the bed. The extra weight would be slow going, even in four-wheel drive.

"They make for a very nice family," Yield said. "Want one myself one day."

"Caleb was an asshole," Cotter said.

"Yeah, she deserves better. You gonna be better?" Yield asked.

"Trying," he mumbled.

"I think your 'try' is far better cry than anything that dude ever 'intended' to do," Yield said. "He took something that he shouldn't have. I suspect that's what got him dead."

"Can I ask what he took?"

"Pictures," Yield said. "Compromising photos of a high-powered political figure."

"Not good," Cotter replied.

"Nope," Yield said. "I will report that the man is dead. No evidence with the wife and kid, but if you find them, or if they are in a P.O. Box or anything else, burn them. Please don't make me have to come back."

"If you come back without an invitation to dinner, I'm going to make sure you never leave this property," Cotter said.

"Understood," Yield said, handing him a card. "Call me for that dinner. I ain't got plans for Christmas. I can take the cot."

A wink and a wave were all Yield gave as he disappeared through the trees. The sun was breaking through the tree line, rising over the creek, as Cotter climbed into the driver's seat and headed towards the house. The 10 point buck's head dangled off the back of the tailgate. He arrived in the front yard to find the Sheriff's truck parked there.

"Just fucking dandy," Cotter said, putting the truck in park. "And now this ass wipe shows up."

# Chapter Eight – Figuring it Out

C otter stomped the snow off his boots before coming in the front door of the house. The warmth inside the domicile welcomed him home, along with a smiling Johnnie, who ran to greet him with hugs and love, and Judy seated behind the table with squinted eyes. He chunked the bloody knife in his hand on the table on top of the mail. Pleased to see the letter Caleb had sent was no longer in the pile, he offered her a hesitant smile. The Sheriff, watching their interaction for signs of lies, fingered the handle on the coffee mug.

"I hope you plan to put that bloody knife in the sink," Judy said to Cotter.

"Oh yeah, sorry," Cotter mumbled. "I cut myself trying to break down the deer to get it in back of my truck. Got a 10 pointer."

"I sure as hell hope you don't plan to gut that thing on the back porch! You will use the dressing shed on the side of the house, Cotter Wihlborg," Judy said defiantly. "I'm guessing you may need to get the fire started in that old stove out there if you plan to make the sausage today while that game is still fresh meat."

His eyes were wide as he looked at the Sheriff, his left hand held down low as he mimicking that she was nagging him by running off at the mouth, his fingers opening and closing like he held an invisible puppet. Sheriff Rottingham tried to hide his laughter, but wanted to get to the bottom of why he'd come out. One, he knew they were lying. Two, he just didn't know about what. Today, he was going to find out.

Cotter too knew the man had done a background check on him as was prepared for any questions the lawman may have. His cover for the job remained rooted in the truth. He couldn't get caught in a lie if there wasn't one to tell. Sitting down at the table, he removed the heavy boots and Johnnie set them by the fire.

"Thanks sweetheart," he told Johnnie.

"You're welcome, Daddy," Johnnie replied. The sound of it made him smile. He liked her calling him that name. It felt right.

"Sheriff, to what do we owe the honor of this visit? I know it's not for Judy's coffee," Cotter said, winking at the woman.

Leaning back in the chair and taking off his hat to reveal a slightly balding head, the Sheriff ran his weathered hand over the smooth skin. Sighing loudly, then taking another sip of coffee, he set the cup down, then adjusted his belting.

The Sheriff sighed again, "I did some checking on you two and I have some questions. I hope you can clarify."

"Sure," Cotter said. "We have nothing to hide; however, I do take exception to you running a background check on me and Judy, but I knew you would. Go ahead."

"It seems this property, or rather the deed to the property, is registered to a Judith, Johnathan and Johnetta Morgan," the Sheriff said, looking at Judy.

"My mother was a jazz singer," she stated. "She also loved the freeness of an artist named Judy Clay, who sang the first racially integrated song with Billy Vera, called *Storybook Children*. I was named after the singer. I am Judith Morgan and that is Johnetta."

She pointed at the child removing her clothing from the inside clothes drying rack above the fireplace mantle.

"Holy crap! That's a girl?" the Sheriff said.

"Yes, I bought this property before my marriage in my maiden name," Judy said. "I knew I was either going to name my first child Johnetta or Johnathan after my father. I named both children ahead of time, so when I give Cotter a son, his name will be Johnathan."

Cotter's eyebrows raised as warmth filled his cheeks. She was a sharp one. He had really begun to not only like her, but appreciate her as well. The rifle, which he'd left in the corner of the room with the silencer, was still there, but missing the silencer. *Good girl.* She'd also folded the sleeping cot and stored it out of sight.

"And where were you two married?" Sheriff Rottingham asked.

"In Vegas, seven years ago," Judith said as Cotter stood, taking the bloody knife to the sink, rinsing it, and then removing his outer jacket and the long-sleeved shirt. The cut on his arm showed from the run-in he had with Yield in the woods. He pulled the shirt over his head, leaving him in just the thick pants and a white tank top undershirt. The scars on his body showed as he poured himself a cup of coffee and rejoined the impromptu inquisition at the table.

"Good. Good," the lawman said, turning his attention to Cotter. "I see your state of residence is in Georgia."

"Yeah, I have a house in Venture. Bought it after I got out of the Army," Cotter said. "I rent it to some college kids in grad school down there."

"Army, huh?"

"Yeah, Special Forces, retired after 20," he said.

"Retired? You don't look old enough to have retired from anywhere," the Sheriff said, leaning forward to take a closer look at the man.

"You can do that after 20 years. I joined at 18, retired at 38 with my pension, and the injuries got me a nice disability check," he said truthfully.

"I guess that's why there's no work history on you for the past 10 years," Rottingham said.

"A Purple Heart gets you all sorts of bennies," Cotter said. "Cost of living in Georgia is pretty low down in Venture. I did odd handyman jobs before heading to Vegas and falling hard for this little lady. Stayed out there for a while with her, then she told me she bought this land. We built this house ourselves."

"No kidding?"

"Solar arrays and all," Cotter said with a smile.

"You seem to be away a lot."

"My folks are still in Minnesota," Cotter offered. "My Mom took ill a few months back, so I went up there to look after some things. Judy here can barely handle this cold, as you see she's sick, so weren't no need to take her and the kid to a frigid place like where I grew up. That kind of cold seeps into your bones and you never feel warm."

The Sheriff watched closely as Judy, who had also removed the bullet he'd taken from Yield's leg and the bloody cloths from the table, move around the kitchen. He could tell she was sick although she tried hard to pretend, she was right as rain. The little woman strolled to the kitchen pantry, which was sadly bare, to collect the first aid kit. Working on his arm in silence, she cleaned the cut and drizzled pure honey into the cut.

"Honey?" Rottingham asked, surprised.

"Best thing to use on cuts, has a million uses," Judy said, wiping away the excess and bandaging the cut.

"Wow, learn something new every day," he said, placing his hat back on his head. "Thanks for the coffee."

"Is that why you came out, Sheriff, to ask us all these questions?" Cotter asked.

"No, my Deputy spotted a strange car coming this way, and I just wanted to check and make sure you folks were all right out here," he said, getting to his feet.

"Appreciate it," Cotter said.

The Sheriff, moving towards the door, spotted the rifle. Lifting it into his hand, he sniffed at the barrel, checking to see if it had been recently fired. Satisfied it had, he nodded, looking again at Johnnie and shaking his head.

"You all have a great day," he said, opening the front door.

Cotter sat, waiting for the sound of the car engine to get started and he grabbed his phone, punching in two digits. He listened quietly, waiting for the person on the other end to answer. Judy, wringing her hands, had a million questions for him, mostly about the Sheriff checking on the status of their marriage. A male voice came through the phone loud and clear.

"Archangel, this is Stop," Cotter said. "I need a marriage license altered from Vegas, registered seven years ago from Caleb Morrow and Judith Morgan to my name, Cotter Wihlborg. I spell, Charlie, Oscar, Tango, Tango, Echo, Romeo. Last name, Whiskey, India, Hotel, Lima Bravo, Oscar, Romeo, Golf."

"Does this mean you have to kill me now that I know your real name?" The Archangel asked through the phone.

"No, but it has to happen fast. I have a Smokey on my heels, a lady and kid in trouble," Cotter said.

"What about the birth certificate for the kid?"

Cotter lowered the phone, looking at Judy. "Where is Johnnie's birth certificate filed? Here in this county?"

"Yes," she said. "Caleb signed it as well."

Into the phone he said, "Rocheport, Missouri, Boone County."

"Got it," Gabriel replied. "My normal fees apply and congrats on your new family. Anything else you need?"

"A prayer would be nice," Cotter said, waiting on Gabriel to pray with, and in this case, for him. The deep voice opened the prayer while Cotter closed his eyes and bowed his head, listening to the strengthening words of the prayer and finally whispering, "Amen."

"I'll get this taken care of now," Gabriel told him.

"Thank you," Cotter said, hanging up the phone.

Judy was staring at him as well as Johnnie. So much to talk about, so much to say. If the person on the other line could do as Cotter asked in a few minutes, he would be on record as her husband and Johnnie's father. On his left hand he wore a ring given to him by his father. A simple gold band, which was the only thing the man really gave him other than his name. It had worked well thus far for their cover. After Gabriel Neary was done, it would be a symbol of their union.

"You do realize what you've just done right?" Judy asked.

"Yep," he said, pulling the shirt over his head and putting it on to head outside. "I'm your husband and that's my daughter. I need to get the fire started in the dressing shed. Nice move letting me know it was there, taking off the silencer, and the clean-up. You're pretty sharp."

"Cotter, we have a lot to discuss," she said, getting to her feet.

"True, but I need to work on that deer first, get that meat ready," he said. "Looking forward to having some sausage for supper. After that, we need to head to Vegas in a day or so. It will do you good to dry out those lungs and we can pick up our marriage license."

"Wait a damned minute! You say it all so casually," she said.

"You asked me to stay, didn't you? So, I'm staying," he said, shoving his feet into the boots by the fireplace. He grabbed his jacket and gloves, looking at her.

"Cotter?" she said softly, feeling suddenly shy. "I'm looking forward to having some sausage too."

He laughed. A loud, gut-busting rumbling laugh as he blew a kiss to Johnnie and made his way out the front door. Picking up an armload of firewood, he slugged through the snow to locate the shed on the side of the house. Opening the door, he was pleased to see the hooks, meat grinder, and even supplies for bagging and casings for making sausages. The shelves were loaded with seasonings and dry spices, and there was even a wench to pull in the kill to hang it from the rafter to clean it. A drain was in the floor for the blood run off and Cotter smiled.

"Shit, everything a man needs is right here on this land," he said, dumping the logs into the potbelly stove and getting the fire started. Cotter was also pleased to locate an unopened box of white freezer wrapping paper sheets for the meat. Letting the shed warm, he slogged through the snow to his truck, ready to drive around to the shed and unload the buck and cut it up. Growing up, he'd learned methods to break down game in less than a few hours, ensuring there was always meat in the freezer in their house. Once he joined the Army, he sent a portion of his check home to help his mother. There were so few times in his life when he'd done a thing for himself.

The woman and child he wanted for himself. At this point, it wouldn't matter if she was lousy in bed, he'd teach her the things he liked as he learned what pleased her in bed as well. Right now, she was sick. He couldn't run the risk of getting sick too. There was too much to do. More than anything, in order for it to work, he needed to tell her the truth.

He only hoped she wouldn't hate him for it.

INSIDE THE HOUSE, A very nervous Judy started Johnnie on a class lesson as she changed the bedding and put on fresh sheets. Tonight, she would share this bed with him. He was also going to need a bath after the whole deer gutting thing.

Catching a glimpse of herself in the mirror, she looked a fright. Her hair was disheveled, her skin was pallid, and her lips were slightly crusty from the dehydration. In three days, he had waltzed his huge ass through her front door and changed everything for her and Johnnie. Love, she told herself, was for school girls. This made sense. They needed protection and he obviously needed to take care of someone. It was a win-win.

A flash of all the men she and Princess had lived with on and off through the years shot across her mind. *I'm no different than my Mama. All these years of self-righteousness, and I still turned into my mother.* Stopping at fluffing the pillows with the fresh new cases, she thought about his phone call, realizing she needed to make one as well.

She placed the call, asking about the order she'd bought plus proof of services provided. Judy gave the operator her new phone number and was told that the information she'd requested had been mailed and she would receive it in a day or so. It would take several weeks to get the death certificate which she needed in order to file the insurance paperwork to get the money.

If Cotter turned out to be an asshole, she would have a rainy-day fund for herself and Johnnie. Sitting on the side of the bed, she only wished that he wouldn't be. Instead, her heart held onto a blind hope that finally, the family she'd always wanted, she'd finally have.

# Chapter Nine – A Quiet Night

Three hours. It took three hours to cut out the good pieces of meat along with the backstrap. Never much caring for the offal, he bagged it up to take it deep in the woods to feed a carnivorous family scratching out a meal in the snow. The shed was a nice touch. It had everything a man needed to get things done and take care of his family. Whoever designed it took into consideration all the small details. The shed even had a dividing wall from the main room that held a toilet and a urinal. A sink, deeply recessed, sat outside the wall to be shared with the processing part of the shed. It was only, in his estimation, 800 square feet of man cave awesomeness. There was even a speaker with an MP3 player connected for tunes.

He didn't care much for the musical selections on the device and opted instead to work in silence. He added chunks of meat to the freshly washed grinder and attached the casings. Adding just enough spice, he began hand-cranking the grinder, watching ribbons of sausage fill the clear casing, twisting as each meat link got to the perfect length. Cotter thought about the kid who lived next door to them in Minnesota. *What was his name? Ralph. Ricky.*

*Ricky!*

Their family was poor like his own. His father, Mike, hunted for their meat. Ricky wasn't the type to take a life. Deer, elk or otherwise. When Cotter asked to learn to hunt, Mike was happy to teach him. Unlike his son Ricky who threw up at the sight of gutting a deer, Cotter didn't balk. The first two times he watched. The third time Mike handed him the knife and showed him how.

At the age of 13, he couldn't get a job to help out around the house, but he could hunt. He took down his first buck in one shot which provided enough meat to last his family for six months. It was a lesson learned. The following season he made sure he shot two deer a season to have enough meat to last until the next season. By the time he was 15, he calculated that if he took down four animals, he could sell the meat from the other two in order to buy pork chops, ham and bacon.

Mike, a connoisseur of venison, explained every season which spices made the best sausage, and how to cook a roast so that it melted in your mouth and didn't taste gamey. Over the years, he'd held on to those tips and his sharp-shooting was what led to him becoming a sniper in the Army. The sharpshooting and quiet methods of getting shit done earned him a spot in the Ranger Regiment, then in Special Forces. He started out taking down deer to feed his family. He wound up taking down bad men under the guise of protecting his country. Finally, he ended up taking out bad decisions made by people with too much money.

Today, he was a married man with a daughter. *I have a family*. A little thing he hadn't planned on since he'd never quite gotten right the whole share his life with a woman thing. He hated being nagged. Bossed around. *Whining*. That's what it was: the whining. Susie, his little sister, whined all the time. Her voice was like nails on a chalkboard to him, and he hated the sound of a woman whining, *expecting* a man to do things for her.

The few women he'd dated, even in the Army, started out tough and hard-core, but in the end, started whining about his socks, his boots, a dirty plate left in the sink. Just to have peace of mind, he lived alone. Living alone, a man could wash a fucking dish when and if he felt like it. His boots, smelly socks, and dirty underwear could grow into a Christmas tree in the corner of the house if he wanted them to, but it wasn't his style.

*Oh shit! A Christmas tree*!

His back ached from hefting the deer into the truck. His arm burned from the cut and working in the tight confines of the deer carcass to get the cuts of meat just so. In a word, he was tired. A nice soak in a hot tub of water would be nice.

*Shit. I need to fix the tub*.

A light tap at the door made him jump. Instinctually, he reached for his weapon. He always kept it on him and pretty close by as he eased his way to the door, cracking it open to find Johnnie standing outside in the bright ass orange coat with a cup of hot coffee.

"Hey kiddo, is that for me?" he asked, not wanting her to see the mangled deer hanging on the hook.

"Yes sir," she said, pushing past him and coming inside the shed. To his surprise, she didn't balk at the bloody mess in the shed. "Mama said you should be getting hungry. She sent coffee and a sandwich. It's sliced chicken."

"Thank you," he said, taking the goodies. "You can take these sausages back inside for me. Give them to your Mom and let her know we'll have them for dinner with some rice."

"Will do," Johnnie said, but she hadn't moved.

"What's on your mind, sweetie?"

Her bundled up little body swayed from side to side as she fought to find the courage to ask the man questions. "You gonna be my Daddy now?"

"Depends on whether or not you are okay with that," he said, as if she had a choice in the matter.

"I'm okay with it," Johnnie replied. "Do I call you Daddy?"

"I would prefer if you called me Pops for now, then when company is around, you can call me Daddy," Cotter said. "You understand?"

"I got it," she said. "Are you a bad man, like my real Daddy?"

Cotter watched the little face, nearly hidden under the cap and hood of the brightly colored coat. She was setting him up for a blow to his chest and he could feel it. This was another of those moments with Johnnie where she gave him just enough information to figure it out.

"What makes you say your Daddy was a bad man?" he asked, drinking the hot coffee, which in his estimation was far too bitter.

"Mama never let him tuck me in at night or give me baths," she said. "She watched you real close with me. Especially when you washed my hair. If you are a bad man, she'll make you disappear too."

"You think your Mama made your Daddy disappear because he did bad things to you?" Cotter asked, concerned.

"My Mama is quiet," Johnnie said, moving around to the deer carcass. "There's a spot over the hill where Mama would dump these after she cleaned the rabbits and does. I never knew her to get a buck. It would be nice to keep this skin to make a rug for my room."

"I'll see what I can do about that," Cotter said, watching the little girl go towards the door.

"She's making water for you to take a bath when you come inside," Johnnie said. "I'll get these sausages to her for dinner."

"Thanks," he said to her. She didn't respond, and he watched the orange coat disappear around the side of the house. His stomach rumbled, pushing him to wash his hands and start on the sandwich. He ate in silence, the thoughts pinging in a head that tried to wrap his mind around what the child had just told him.

*Did she open the contract on Caleb? How, she is flat broke? Or is she? No phone. No power. No way to get to town to buy food.*

His hackles were up as he wolfed down the sandwich, which sat in his stomach like a lump of coal. Finishing up the processing, he filled a bucket with water to wash the blood down the drain. The antlers he kept, along with the hide, but the remainder he put in large bags and took to his truck. Over the hill the kid said. Three armloads of meat were carried into the house and set on the table. The tub, filled with just enough water, beckoned him but he needed to discard the offal and items and ensure no embers were left in the potbelly stove.

"Be back in a jiffy," he said, going to the shed to secure it and double check behind himself. The hide, he left hanging, but the rest of the place was clean.

Outside, he looked over the land and saw only one hill. Sludging his way to the truck, he cranked it and made for the hillside. Shifting to a lower gear, the heavy-duty truck climbed the embankment with ease. Carefully, he unloaded the bag, opening the top to allow the scent of blood to fill the air for hungry diners. Looking down the hillside, the snow-covered area prevented him from seeing the years of bones underneath the piles of compacted powder.

He dumped the contents, taking the bloody bag with him, but as he turned, a gust of wind hit hard in his face, blurring his vision. Blinking away the tears, his eyes slowly focused and his breath caught. The land, covered in snow, reminded him of a Christmas card. The small home at the bottom of the hill had on two lights and the billowing of smoke from the chimney. He imagined in the summer, the green hillside covered in wildflowers that he would pick to bring home to the woman, who in turn would teach the girl to dry the petals for other uses.

A tightness hit him as he held his chest, thinking, she was waiting for him. The bath he knew was her way of saying tonight she would give herself to him, to become his wife in every sense of the word. He wanted that more than anything. Shaking off the bevy of emotions, grey shadows appeared in the wood line of hungry wolves coming to feed. His moment of nostalgia rudely interrupted, Cotter got to his feet. Inside his truck, he held the steering wheel, then downshifted to a lower gear and made his way home.

*Home.*

Driving down the hill he had a thought. A silly thought but it would be a nice surprise and gift. Far enough away from the feeding wolves, he stopped the truck. The one upside to his type of work was that in his truck he held all the tools of his trade and a few others for just in case situations. He stopped the truck, climbing out, his feet covered in the depth of untouched snow. Opening the rear door, he lifted the back seat to take out a handy tool, which was ideal for the task at hand. Smiling, he went to work to bring his ladies home the perfect gift. *Home.* He whispered to himself and set about the job at hand.

COTTER CAME THROUGH the front door dragging a four-foot-tall pine tree that he'd shaken the snow off the branches, tapping it lightly on the front porch and stepping inside. His chest poked out with pride as he leaned the lopsided shortleaf pine against the wall. Wide eyes watched the man, grinning from ear to ear with the Charlie Brown looking Christmas tree which he presented as if he'd conquered the world, Paul Bunyan style.

"Oh, it's a Christmas tree," Johnnie said.

"I'm hoping you have decorations for it, if not, Johnnie and I can head into town after dinner and grab some cranberries to string," Cotter said. "If you have needle and thread, I bought a bag of corn we could pop and string that too."

"String cranberries and popcorn?" Judy asked, slightly confused as to why he would want to put food on strings in a Christmas tree.

"Yeah, we would string cranberries and popcorn for garland each year," he said. "It was cost efficient and gave us something to do to keep us out of Mom's hair. I mean, unless you already have ornaments."

"We have ornaments, but you, Mister, smell like something the dog dragged in to play with and are in dire need of a bit of soap and water," Judy said.

"Pops, you smell terrible," Johnnie said, picking up the bar of soap. "We got your bath water started too."

"Thanks a lot, both of you," he said, bending to unlace his boots. Cotter kicked them off and hung his jacket on the hook by the door. The outer shirt was removed as he kept his eyes on Judy who carried a hot pot of water to the waiting tub. Johnnie disappeared, returning with his towel and washcloth, plus his lounge pants and a clean tee shirt. It was his last one. Tomorrow, he would have to wash and buy a few more items. He only traveled with five days' worth of clothing, and now he was down to his last.

"I'm going to my room," Johnnie said, leaving them alone.

"I'll let you know when he's done," Judy said.

"Hopefully, dinner will be done too," Johnnie countered, "because I'm hungry."

"When is that kid not hungry?" Cotter asked, removing his shirt and pants to step into the warm water. He lowered his body into the tub, leaning against the side, stretching his legs over the rim, allowing the warm water to soothe his back. He groaned in satisfaction as the water pooled around his waist.

Judy, carrying a small glass container, spooned lavender-scented salts into the water as she looked at the strong face. His eyes were closed and his long lashes lay spread out against the weathered skin. The contentment on his face was enough for her to take a seat and just look at him. Handsome. Rugged. Broken.

"I know you are relaxing, but I have some concerns," she said softly. His eyelids didn't flutter nor his face give an expression. "You have done so much for us, and I'm grateful; however, everything has a price. I'm waiting for you to tell me yours. What is it that you get out of all of this? What is it you want me to do for you or to give you?"

"Johnathan," he said, sighing loudly.

"What?" she asked, unclear as to his meaning.

"You said you had two children's names picked out to inherit this land, a girl and a boy named Johnathan," Cotter said. "Give me a son and we can round out our family."

Judy sat on the couch, just watching his face. One eye opened suddenly making her jump in place. *A son. He wants me to give him a son.*

"Have you changed your mind, Judy?"

"No, I thought we were just putting on a show for the Sheriff," she said.

"But you have the boy's name already," Cotter countered, "and it's on the deed to the property. Give me Johnathan. I will be happy."

"Is that all you want is a son? Cotter, what about the rest?"

"The rest of what?" he asked, sitting up in the water. His eyes bore into her with an intensity that made her shudder.

"I'm no fool to believe that you and I will be some kind of love match, that we made the choices which landed us here. I just don't plan to be alone out here again, waiting for a man to come to my rescue if you decide to leave," she said softly.

"When my truck leaves this property, both of you will be in it with me," he said. "Speaking of that, I think we should take the train to Vegas from Kansas City. It is about the same distance driving as taking the train. At least with the train, I don't have to spend so much time behind the wheel and we can get a sleeping car."

"Cotter, you changed the subject on me again," she said wistfully. "We need to discuss things. Understand how this is going to work out for us both."

"Easy, we both get what we want—a family," he said, leaning back in the tub. "Hey, will you wash my back again for me?"

"I'm going to drown you in that damned tub if we don't have a conversation about how this is going to work for us as a family," she said, emphasizing the word family.

"I go out, hunt, kill, and bring home the bread," he said. "You butter it, buy pretty stuff for the house, and together we raise a family."

"You said the kill portion too easy," she muttered. "Is that what you do for a living?"

"Do you really want to know...tonight?"

"Not really," she said, "But I need to know how you make a living. How you came across Caleb, what he sent you here to do."

Cotter bolted upright in the tub again. *The box. The fucking box.* "He sent me to bring you a box. I didn't open it, so I have no idea what's in it."

"How did you happen to come across him as he was dying, as a matter of fact where did he die and how did he die?" she asked, wringing her hands together. "Was it by your hand?"

He didn't want to start his new life off the same way the old one ended, with a lie. He wanted more than anything to be truthful with her, but the uncertainty of her reaction he wasn't prepared for. Instead, he employed the oldest tactic in the book, feeling like an ass for doing so, but now just wasn't the right time to confess his sins.

"Seriously? I go out, hunt down enough meat to feed you, the kid and two neighbors for at least three months, and this is the thanks I get? I even made sausage and cut down a fucking tree as a present. Maybe you're right. This isn't going to work," he said, sounding exasperated. "The last thing I need in my life is a nagging, ungrateful woman. Fine, I will fix what I can and move on, but just remember, you made the offer for me to stay."

"And I want you to stay, but I have every right to know if the husband I am laying down with tonight is the same one who killed the last man I was married to!" she said, throwing the Caleb tactic back in his face. Too many years of dealing with Princess' ne'er-do-wells had taught her to spot a pile and shit and then say it stank.

"At this point will it matter?"

"Everything matters, Cotter," she said softly. "Everything we do in this life to each other and against each other matters."

"You were half starved and dying when I walked through those doors, and now you are on your feet and full of piss and vinegar. Maybe that's why he left," Cotter said.

She was on her feet and coming at him. The first slap he wasn't prepared for, catching him off guard. The second blow he caught in his hand, yanking her into the tub with him. Face to face they stared at each other, both breathing hard. Unable to stop himself, he pulled her to him, kissing her hard on the mouth, expecting her to fight, but she didn't. Her body went all soft against him, as she parted her lips for a deeper kiss.

"Shit," he mumbled, trying to drag his mouth away. The taste of honey on her tongue from the tea made the kisses even sweeter and at the peril of getting sick himself, he didn't give a sneeze in the middle of a blizzard, he was kissing her back.

"You got me all wet," she said breathily into his mouth.

"Just getting started, little lady," he said, pushing her out of the tub and getting to his feet. Wet ass, dry feet, and hard on to rival his teen years, he yanked her by the hand to the bedroom. Cotter locked the door as he eyeballed the turned down bed with freshly made sheets. She'd prepared for this night.

He had as well.

# Chapter Ten – Blind Hope

Judy snatched her hand out of his grip and leaned against the wooden door. The exasperation of the whole week had worn her down more than the lungs filled with phlegm. She wanted him to understand she was grateful for all that he'd done for them, but she wasn't ready to be married again to a man that she didn't know. She'd learned her lesson with Caleb. Repeating the behavior with this man was foolish.

"Cotter, please slow down, we need to talk," she said, watching his firm backside go to the bed and comfortably seat itself.

"What is there to talk about? This morning you said you wanted some sausage, I have sausage. Don't you like mine?" he asked pointing to the erection demanding her attention.

"It's a very nice sausage, but you have been moving so fast, plus I'm sick, and we haven't talked about a great deal of things," she said, rubbing down the wet skirt. Judy realized she needed to get out of it, unzipping the ankle length skirt and removing the material. Her blouse too was wet and the last thing she needed was to get sicker than she already had been. The pills he'd been giving her worked wonders, but she wasn't out of the woods.

"Judy, come on," he said, twisting his lips. "We can talk later, unless you are trying to tell me you are bad in bed. Are you a dud in bed, Judy? If so, we can work with it."

"Noooo," she said, wide eyes. "I am not a dud in bed. Can we focus please, Cotter?"

"Oh, so you are telling me that you're hot stuff in bed and that I am going to be shocked at your limberness and acrobatic abilities?" he said with a waggle of his eyebrows. Cotter fell back on the bed, his legs splayed wide, his index finger beckoning her over.

"Can you please focus?"

"I am focused! This morning you said you wanted sausage, and I'm ready, but now you want to play coy and talk about your feelings. Hell, let's talk about mine," he said. "I'm feeling some kind of way and have been looking forward to this all day and now, you are saying no. What the hell, Judy?"

"I'm not saying no, Cotter, I'm just trying to get us to discuss some very important matters here. About you and me, and there's Johnnie to consider," Judy protested, now down to her damp undies and wet bra.

"I hear what you are saying, Judy, but at this point I don't really give a shit," he said. "Just today alone, I put a bullet in a 150+ lb. deer so you would have meat for six months. I put a bullet in a man who was probably going to torture you for information that you don't even have. I lied to an officer of the law. To make matters worse, I paid good money to have legal documents forged in order to protect you and Johnnie, which made me husband and father in one fell swoop. Fuck, I even made sausage by hand and cut down a goddamned tree for Christmas. What the hell do I have to do in order to get some reciprocity in this bitch? Besides, I didn't even ask you for it, you offered. I accepted. Forgive me for having a bit of blind hope that all of this would work out, but none of that matters right now. Right now, I need for you, my wife, to either get your ass over here and take care of me, or get your ass over here and take care of this!" he pointed at the angry throbbing erection almost blinding him from all logic and reasoning.

"Fine!" she said, filled with anger for him not wanting to listen to what she had to say. She removed the wet undies and bra, tossing them to the floor and moving to the bed. "I hope you catch whatever I have."

"Just make sure you throw it hard enough for me to feel it was worth my damned time and effort lady," Cotter said, feeling more excited than he had in years as she climbed on the bed.

Cool fingers encircled the throbbing erection as he sighed in relief at her touch. The other hand cupped the life givers, gently massaging as he closed his eyes, trying to think of anything he could so he wouldn't embarrass himself by letting go too soon. Her grip tightened as she commenced to massaging the powerful tool up and down as his breath caught in his throat. The heat from her mouth as it touched the sensitive tip nearly made him come off the bed.

Judy realized it had been a while for him just in his reactions to her touch. A man who received 'attention' on a regular basis didn't react this way to the initial stages of foreplay. He wanted her to take care of him. It was the least she could do, considering her need for what was about to occur was equal if not greater than his own. Losing herself in the moment, she treated his body as if he were the last man capable of reproduction on the planet.

Cotter bit down on his lips as her mouth worked him over. Clutching at the bed covers, he reached for a pillow to shove in his mouth to keep from yelling out like Tarzan. It was good. Damned good, but he didn't have any reserves in him as he blindly reached for her, pulling her naked body away as the suction sound of her mouth leaving him made him throb even more.

"Enough. I want you," he said, pulling her body atop his own. He struggled with her legs, positioning him over her, pointing, aiming and gently pushing into the warm opening. It was a snug fit, but he planned to take his time.

"Goodness," she said, leaning forward, the perfectly sized, small ebony breasts, pressing against his chest. The narrow hips moved slowly, trying to take him all in. "You feel good."

"Ditto," he mumbled, allowing his rough hand to run down the smooth skin. Cupping her bottom, he craved the need to have her speed up. He was right there and ready. Needing the release like a cold glass of water on a hot muggy day, he encouraged her to move. "Get me there, Judy. Take care of me."

She needed no other words as she began rocking her hips up and down. The feel of the thickness sliding in and out turned her on to the point she nearly forgot the child was in the house. Leaning forward, she grabbed a handful of his hair, whispering in his ear, "This is mine. You're mine, Cotter Wihlborg, from this day forward, 'til death do us part."

"Sure, sure, whatever you want, lady," he said, focusing on the sensations, the pleasure, her enjoyment of him. The bed squeaked as she gyrated low into his hips then high, and coming to her feet. Her hands rested on his chest for balance as she worked him in and out of the dampness of her body. His eyes were wide, watching the throbbing hot rod disappear into her dark skin, her movements amazing him. Then she started to twitch.

"Oh, my goodness," she said, feeling the start of her climax. "This is so fucking good. So good."

She worked her hips, moving faster and faster, her body clamping tight around him. Her nails grazed his skin as she rocked fast and hard, whispering his name, riding him for all he was worth. Judy flung her head back as he licked his thumb, searching through the thick mass of girl curls, locating the nub of flesh and rubbing it quickly. He could feel the explosion inside of her as she let go. Getting close himself, he sat up on the bed and rolled her over to her back.

He buried himself as deep as he could go and thrust hard. She whimpered against his cheek. Her hot breath fueled him as he pumped, deep, deeper still until he was there.

"Say my name, Judy," he said to her. "Tell me this is yours again. Tell me, dammit!"

"You're mine, Cotter Wihlborg, you're mine!" she moaned, clamping her legs around his hips, encouraging him to give her more.

Cotter let go. Years of late-night connections with faces he didn't want to see in the morning all vanished. He wanted to see her face in the morning, the evening, and all damned day long if he had his way. She said he was hers.

For the first time in his life, he believed a woman.

"Damn!" he grunted as he let loose months of pent up aggression, hatred, and frustration. He body slid across the bed as he pumped her so hard that he almost feared he would snap her into, but there was no way to stop what he was giving her. She shifted his body to come to his knees as he thrust repeatedly, filling Judy with his hot seed. His right leg shook as he collapsed on top of her, sated.

"That was amazing," Judy said, rubbing his hair. Hot breath, followed by a fit of coughs ensued as she pushed at his chest, to get him off of her so she could clean up and get dressed.

"Not just yet," he said into the side of her neck then rolled to his back, taking her with him. "Let me hold you for a moment."

In silence, they lay in bed, filled with words which needed to be said, but he was right. This was not the time.

OVER DINNER, QUIETLY they ate sausages simmered with onions over a bed of rice with a green salad. Johnnie monopolized the conversation about Christmas ornaments and the need to go shopping for presents. She also chose this time to barter for more allowance.

"You are giving her an allowance?" Judy asked, surprised.

"She gets 10 bucks, but I didn't say how often," Cotter said.

"I think it should be a week, that way I will have enough to buy each of you a present," Johnnie said with pride.

"Well, first we have to get packed and get to St. Louis to make the train," Cotter said.

"We are really going?" Johnnie said getting to her feet. "We are really going to take the train to Las Vegas? If I had friends, this is when I would call them to brag. I'm so excited I can't stand it!"

Cotter looked at Judy, squinting his eyes. "Yeah, she needs to get out more."

"So, does her Mama," she said, looking at him and seeing a different man. A relaxed man. A man who seemed to be a bit more at peace. "Only thing is, I am flat broke. Hey, you said Caleb sent a box to us?"

"Oh yeah, let me go and get it," Cotter said, eating the last of the sausage on his plate.

"What do you think it is, Mama?"

"I hope it something good," she said with a forced smile.

Cotter went out to the truck, returning moments later with the box. It was locked and Caleb had not given him a key with which to open it. Judy didn't have one either, but it was Johnnie who laughed.

"I have the key," she said, running to her room to retrieve the skeleton key her Daddy had given her before he left.

"If you have the key maybe you should open it," Cotter said.

"No, I don't think that's a good idea," Judy replied, taking the key from her daughter who took it back, clutching it to her chest.

"Daddy sent the box and only I have the key. He meant for me to open it," Johnnie said defiantly. She looked to Cotter for reinforcement of her decision, and he nodded his head. Both he and Judy held their breath as she inserted the key, turning it, freeing the hasp. The box opened, and her eyes grew wide. Judy anxious, turned the box around to see a manila envelope sitting atop a pile of cash.

"Must be at least 25 grand in that box," Cotter said, more interested in the envelope which Judy opened, then frowned. Reaching for the envelope, Cotter glanced at the photos of the well-known Senator, who preached marriage vows and righteousness, in copulation with a woman who wasn't his wife. He saw no need to look any further into the envelope but took it to the fireplace and threw it on the embers.

"He sent back the money he took from me," Judy said softly.

Johnnie, not missing a beat, grinned. "This means my allowance is going to be more than 10 bucks! I can get some really nice Christmas presents for you guys with this!"

"Sweetie, I'm sure your Daddy meant for you to share it with your Mama," Cotter said.

"Uh-uh! I have the key, so it's mine," Johnnie said, "but I will share."

They laughed as Johnnie went to find paper and pencils for her new parents to make their Christmas lists. Over the table, Cotter and Judy shared knowing glances, wanting the tree trimming to be over so they could all go to bed. Tomorrow would be a big day. Tonight, was going to be special as well.

"This is going to be the best Christmas ever!" Johnnie said happily.

"I think she just might be right," Cotter said, reaching across the table to give Judy's hand a squeeze. Tonight, would be all about the loving and their weekend all about Johnnie. On Monday, with the marriage certificate in hand, he would tell her the truth.

*I just hope she can forgive me.*

# Chapter Eleven – Truth Be Told

In the twilight hours of the morning, Cotter snuggled close to the woman, loving the feel of her body next to his, thinking for the first time in his life, he was actually content. He would move heaven and earth to hold onto this no matter the cost. *I have a family. She will bear me a son. Here is where we will raise them on this land, but man, this house needs some work.* In his head, he made a mental list of all the repairs and upgrades he would add to the homestead. At some point, he would need to take a few jobs to ensure they had enough money for annual vacations and to buy his family the things they needed.

*I will worry about that stuff later.*

JUDY WASN'T ASLEEP. She needed to talk to Cotter about so many things yet he always changed the subject when she tried. It would be a two-hour drive to St. Louis to take the train. She'd never traveled by train before or a road trip in a car. True, she and Caleb had driven from Las Vegas to Rocheport in a rented Winnebago, but a road trip in a vehicle was new. A mini vacation before Christmas.

She tingled all the way to her toes in excitement. She thought herself an idiot for falling so fast for a man she didn't even know, but she didn't care. Cotter was hers. Her husband. They were going to pick up the paperwork that said as much.

*Please don't regret this. Please don't regret this.* Sighing loudly, she drifted off to sleep.

JOHNNIE WAS AWAKE AND packing her small suitcase. In the closet, she put away the extra ornaments from the tree and set bowls on the table for oatmeal for breakfast. Anxious, she ran to the bedroom door, not bothering to knock, bursting into the room. She bounced on the bed, encouraging her newly united parents to get up so they could get moving.

"Johnnie, what time is it?" Judy asked.

"The little hand is on the six and the big hand is on the five," she said. "Get up, we have to get ready. Eat. You guys need to pack. We are going to Las Vegas! I don't know where that is, or what it is, but I want to go!"

"Fine! Fine!" Cotter said, sitting up and wiping the sleep from his eyes.

"Yay!" she said excitedly, showing off her row of tiny teeth. "Vacation! I've never been on one, but I have seen it on television."

"We have to get her some friends, enroll her in dance classes, art classes, or something," Cotter said.

"I couldn't agree with you more," Judy said. "Teach me to drive and help me get my license, then she can get out of this house."

"Yes, ma'am," he said, throwing back the covers and looking for his shoes. Most of his personal items were in storage in Georgia, but nothing he couldn't live without. Other items he would replace as he went along, leaving the tools of his trade in the truck which was a modified home office. "The train leaves at four and it's a two-hour drive. I figured we will get into Vegas about three in morning on Sunday. Head to the Records Department on Monday to get what we need and head back out on Tuesday night. That will put us back here by Thursday night."

"You really know the schedule by heart," Judy said, squinting her eyes.

"Best way to travel if you don't want to be seen," Cotter said, leaving her alone in the bedroom with her thoughts as he made his way to the bathroom.

"I guess you've spent a lot of your life not wanting to be seen," she said to the air. He didn't bother to respond. Judy wanted to call him out on it, but his phone rang. Reaching for it, she picked it up to take it to the owner, but Cotter was in the room lifting it from her hand.

He looked at the caller ID and answered the phone. "Stop," he said into the phone.

"Your documentation is complete," Gabriel Neary said. "When do you plan to pick it up?"

"Headed that way. We will have it on Monday," he replied.

"When you headed back out?"

"Tuesday," Cotter said, not giving any specifics.

"Good enough, pay the bill," Gabriel said.

"Will do and thanks," Cotter said, ending the call. To Judy, "Never answer my phone. Do you understand?"

"I was only going to bring it to you," she said.

"Just remember, never answer it, even if my Mother's picture pops up on the screen," he said.

"Fine, yeesh," she said, turning her back to him. Cotter caught her by the arm. "Judy, I work for some not so nice people. They don't know about you or the kid. It's best they don't."

"I guess you won't be adding us to your insurance plan," she said sarcastically.

"I can add you to my military insurance, not The Company one," he said, looking at her.

"What do you do for a living, Cotter?"

"I take hard jobs, skip traces kind of," he said, taking a seat on the side of the bed.

"And the name, Stop?"

"It means the buck stops with me," he replied. "Clients who are hard to locate are my specialty. I find them and make them pay their debts."

"Is that how you met Caleb?"

There it was. The conversation he'd been dreading. If he told her now, the whole family trip thing would be ruined. It was important to him to give both the woman and Johnnie fresh air and sunshine and the bright lights of Las Vegas. He wanted to get dressed up and take them to dinner and a show. Gamble a bit, make a few extra bucks to maybe buy her a car that was reliable. Telling her now would ruin everything.

"Kind of," he said, standing. "I didn't finish my bath. I want to look at that shower before we go, in case I need to get a whole new tub and enclosure in St. Louis. It will be cheaper there."

"Avoiding the truth is just like telling a lie," she told him.

"Tell me about it, Judy," he said. "Johnnie said you make bad people disappear, is that what you did with Caleb? If I do a thing to displease you, will you make me vanish as well?"

He'd done it again. He had turned the tables on her, leaving her speechless. She stood in the bedroom, wearing the threadbare nightgown, just staring at him.

"Thought so," he said, leaving the room again.

"Cotter, if we can't be truthful with each other, then this will never work," she called after him.

He popped his head around the corner, smiling at her. "When you're ready to tell me the truth, I will do the same."

THE BETTER PART OF the morning was spent fighting with the shower and tub. It leaked like a sieve, forcing him to realize that the whole thing was a bust. He would need to remove all of it and install a new one. The frustration over the bath situation was levied by Johnnie's enthusiasm.

At 11 am, they loaded in the truck and headed towards town. He stopped at the Sheriff's office to let him know they would be gone for a few days and to drive by the place to keep an eye on it. The Sheriff said he was happy to oblige, Cotter gave a nod, and they were on their way.

Johnnie talked non-stop for the first hour. Judy and Cotter were grateful for the silence when she slept the second hour until they finally pulled into Gateway Station in St. Louis. She popped up in the back seat like a meerkat, looking left and right and asking a million questions in the loud orange coat, drawing too much attention to them. Judy whispered in her ear, and the exuberance subsided into a quiet child. Tickets in hand, they located their sleeping car and closed the door. Judy unpacked their things, pulling out board games to occupy the child, along with coloring books with too few pages left to color and crayons which were down to the nubs.

He would get her more for Christmas along with a few paints, easels, and coloring pads. The train rolled along, gently rocking through the midwestern countryside creating a peaceful cocoon in the car until Judy's phone rang. Everyone jumped at the sound. Her hands shook as she took the call.

"Mrs. Morrow, the death certificate is now available in Henderson, Nevada," the voice said. "This completes our transaction for services. We thank you for using The Company to take care of your needs."

"Thank you," she said as the call ended.

"Everything okay?" Cotter asked, not knowing anyone had the number of the new cell phone he'd purchased for her.

"Death notification," she said. "It appears that Caleb's certificate of death is available in Henderson, Nevada."

Her eyes met Cotter's. They were filled with suspicion as a sinking feeling hit them both. Both certificates would be able to be picked up at once. At his encouragement, he had her bring the original marriage certificate with them. *He knew. He knew where Caleb had died which meant he also knew where they had been married.* She fisted her hands, remaining silent for the remainder of the trip.

Cotter had nothing to say either. After dinner in Las Vegas, he would confess all his sins and let the truth be told. Either she would love the man she married or want nothing to do with him. He sat silently watching the child play. Getting to his feet, he left the train car to go to the bar. Never really a smoker, he purchased a cigar, puffing on it lightly while he made a plan with the two of them in his life and a backup plan in case, she never wanted to see him again.

THE TRAIN ARRIVED AT McCarran International Airport at 3:15 in the morning. Rested, but feeling sluggish, they walked through the terminal to the cabbie stands to secure a ride to the Treasure Island Hotel where he'd booked them for their stay. He had opted not to rent a car for such a short turn around, and the cabs would suffice for what they had to do.

Johnnie's excitement over the hotel's pirate theme was enough for him as a start. Checking in, he left the child to her mother's care as he headed straight for a hot shower, then the bed. He slept like a log, not feeling the light weight of her body when she lay down next to him. Only a few words were exchanged between them during the train ride and the journey to the hotel. First thing was first.

He needed sleep.

THE SUN SHONE BRIGHTLY through the window as he woke and ordered room service for breakfast to get their day going. The cool reception continued even when they left the hotel. Often frequenting Las Vegas, the hitman had a few friends in the city of flashing lights. He'd called in a favor to an Uber driver who would be at their service during the remainder of the stay.

Their first stop was to the Division of Vital Records to obtain the death certificate. Judy produced the marriage license and ordered two copies of Caleb's death certificate. It took less than 30 minutes to certify her as the man's widow, then down the hall, she requested copies of her marriage license to a man that left her with entirely too many questions.

To lighten the mood, their Uber driver, John Handy, which she doubted was his real name, dropped them off at the Fashion Show Mall.

"This is most magical place in the world," Johnnie exclaimed as she made a beeline for the Disney Store.

"No, Disneyland is the most magical place in the world," Cotter corrected.

"Will you take me there as well, Daddy?" she asked in front of the sales lady.

It tugged at his heart, nearly making his eyes water as he took to a knee in front of her.

"Nothing would make me happier, sweetheart, than to do that," he said with a smile.

"You have a beautiful family," the store clerk said to him, making his chest swell with pride. Judy also offered a weak smile to the young woman, who helped her daughter select a Princess Tiana suitcase, dress, and a lightweight jacket with pretty blue flowers on it.

While at the mall, Cotter purchased a black suit, a new dress for Judy, and a cute outfit for Johnnie. The simple gold band on her hand from Caleb irritated him and he drug her into a jewelry store. After outfitting her hand with new wedding rings and a solitaire diamond, he was pleased. Judy, not wanting to admit it the sentiment was a nice one and her first actual diamond, which also pleased her. As the hours waned, the Uber driver returned taking them back to the hotel, where they showered, changed and prepared for dinner.

"I feel like a princess," Johnnie commented as she twirled around the floor in the adorable dress, white tights, and shiny black shoes. "Mama, you look so pretty!"

Cotter turned to see her in the sleek black dress, the diamond shining on her finger and just enough lipstick to make him long for time alone with her.

"You look stunning," he said, offering her a smile.

"Not too shabby yourself," she said, fixing his tie.

"Shall we?" he offered, and they left the room, heading out for dinner. "We will talk after dinner and Johnnie goes to bed. No decisions until after we talk, okay?"

"Okay," she said, taking his arm.

# Chapter Twelve – To Have and To Hold....

Judy ate each shrimp with delicate precision, savoring the taste of fresh seafood in her mouth. The crab legs she cracked like a pro, pulling out the succulent white meat as her eyes rolled up in her head with each bite. Johnnie seemed happy to eat chicken with carrots and steamed broccoli and Cotter watched them in amusement. Several diners observed the small family, amazed that a child Johnnie's age actually ordered the vegetables and ate them.

He expected them to order lavish desserts, but instead, they both opted for chocolate ice cream; two scoops each. Johnnie, providing the waitress with a large and overly charming smile, asked for sprinkles to be added to hers, and Cotter gorged himself on a large slice of carrot cake.

"You have a beautiful family," the waiter said. "You daughter looks a lot like you."

"That's what they say happens when you feed them, they start to look like you," Cotter replied, settling the check.

Johnnie held both their hands, walking in the middle of them as they left the restaurant and walked over the bridge to the hotel. The silence between husband and wife palpable, but smoothed over by Johnnie, amazed at the people who looked like statues but were actually moving. Her daughter was happy and vibrant. Judy on the other hand, was torn. She wanted all of this on a regular basis and a life with him, but she needed the truth. If he couldn't be truthful with her, then there was no need to continue the charade. Her lips remained pursed as they climbed into the elevator. The cough, almost gone and she almost felt normal. He was right, the desert air had done wonders for her in such a short period of time. Cotter opened the hotel room door for a twirling Johnnie who grinned from ear to ear.

"This has been the best day of my life!" Johnnie exclaimed, kicking off her shoes in the hotel room. "I love, love, love having you as my Daddy!"

"Get dressed for bed, honey, and I will come and tuck you in," Judy said, turning to look at her husband, married to her on paper. "You son of a bitch!

Was that your plan, win the child over to make it difficult for me to cut your ass loose?"

"Yeah, it was," he said. "I don't want to leave and you don't want me to go either. So, say what's on your mind."

"I want the truth, Cotter," she said. "Tell me the fucking truth about your relationship with my husband, how he died, and why he sent you to us. He didn't send you for this. I deserve some honesty."

Johnnie walked out of the room, her eyes wide. "Mama, what's wrong?"

"Nothing baby, let me tuck you in," she said, following the child to the second bedroom.

Cotter undid his tie and grabbed a mini bottle of the first thing he saw from the bar. Opening the glass container, he poured half into a cup, followed by a splash of Coke. He took a seat on the couch, loosening his tie a bit more. Swallowing the contents in one gulp, he made himself another and waited her return. The fight had left him. Adding a period to make bad people permanently stop was no longer his path. What he needed going forward was her as his wife and that child who called him Daddy. He inhaled as the bedroom door opened and she stepped out, looking for him.

Cotter handed her the glass and patted the seat next to him. Judy took the drink and sat forlornly, giving him the side eye. She took a sip of the drink which was too strong for her and passed it back.

"Are you ready to talk?"

"Yep," he said, taking a drink from the glass.

"How did you know Caleb?"

Sighing deeply, he said, "I am a skip tracer of sorts. Caleb did a bad thing to someone who wanted him tracked down and made to pay for the wrong he'd done. I tracked him down. I made him pay."

"You killed my husband?" she asked incredulously.

"I closed an open contract," he said. "In the end, I stayed with him as he transcended, but before he left, he asked me to bring you the box. I didn't open it, but knowing what I did about the man, concern for any woman who had married him, plus the child, became a priority. Finding you and the kid in that freezing house, starving, did something to me. I don't regret closing the contract. A man who leaves his wife and kid in that state doesn't deserve my pity."

"Why did you stay?"

"You guys needed someone," he said. "You needed a man to make you his priority. A year on the road, I had nothing to go back to. Nothing to look forward to in my life. You gave me a purpose. I love being with you two. If you can forgive me, I want to stay. If you can't, I understand."

Judy touched his hand. "I can forgive you."

It was too easy. She couldn't simply forgive the man who'd taken her husband's life. Then it dawned on him.

"You opened the contract, didn't you?"

Swallowing hard, she lowered her head. "Yes, I did."

"I knew it!" he said loudly, slapping his knee and spilling the drink.

"How did you know it?"

"The phone calls, the money," Cotter said. "You paid the 50 and he took the rest. Where did you get that kind of cash?"

"I worked here in Vegas," she said. "First in Atlantic City, saving every dime I could get my hands on. I spent a chunk of it on the land and the materials to build the house, but that is my home. I love that house."

"That house is a death trap," he said.

"Yes, but it is all we have," she said. "My mother, the con artist, never had anything until her final years. She was so used to hustling that she couldn't for the life of her soul stop and enjoy the bounty she'd finally received. She died penniless with her throat cut, by whom, I still don't know. I didn't want that for my child or me. I also didn't want Caleb Morrow as my husband."

"Please tell me what he did so bad that you had him skip traced. I need to make sure I don't do the same damned thing," Cotter said.

"He lied to me," she said.

"That is no reason to make a man vanish," Cotter said.

"He lied consistently about everything until whatever he touched turned to shit," she said breathing deeply. "I caught him one night in Johnnie's room. She was only about 4 at the time. He was helping her get dressed and taking entirely too long. It sickens me at what I saw. I couldn't have him around our daughter."

"Did he...?"

"No, but her panties were off and he was aroused."

"Shit."

"I put in a call to Jimmy the Flint to get him a gig, but then the month turned into six, the calls home had women in the background and then someone sent me a photo of him with an underage girl," she said. "That's when I made up my mind. I had a policy on him that had a double indemnity clause. If his death was an accident, I would get $1.5 million."

"So, when you turn in the death certificate to the insurance company, you will be rich," he said.

"Hey, you are $50,000 fatter for your efforts," she said.

"True, but where does this leave us, Judy?"

"Cotter, I feel stupid for saying this, but I don't want you to leave," she said. "I want a life with you. Color me stupid for loving you, but I do."

"Glad to hear it, because if you didn't, I was going to find a way to make you," he said, leaning over to kiss her. "I love having a family. You as my wife and my adorable spunky daughter have changed everything for me. That and a hot shower."

"So, we are doing this? Man and wife?"

"And kid, or kids, in a house powered by the sun," he said. "This summer, I will take you to meet my family. My niece finishes at Northwestern in May, so we will go to her graduation."

"You promised Johnnie you'd take her to Disney World," she added as if they hadn't discussed her paying to have her husband killed and him fulling the wish.

"Depends on whether or not you are too fat with my son to travel," he said, touching her tummy.

"Just like a man to want to walk in the door and get somebody pregnant. I just spent two years locked away. I want to drive, travel, and have some damned fun first," she said.

"And you can do all those things, but promise me, we won't wait too long," he said.

"The way you were going at me a few nights ago, I probably already am," she replied.

"I wasn't too rough, was I?" he responded, his voice laced with concern.

"No, not even close. You are lucky I am still sick," she said. "if not, I would have worked your ass over."

"Hell, where are them pills?" he said jumping to his feet. His movements were halted by a knock at the door. Instinct kicked in as he ran in the other room for his weapon. She hid behind the couch as he stood away from the door.

The actions were too normal for them both. He thought as fucked up as all of it was, she was probably the perfect woman for him, as long as he didn't disappoint her. If his life were to end, he didn't want to look up and see One Way coming in his direction. That man didn't care how you died, but one way or another, you were leaving this world, by his hand or an ostensibly creative method of transcending the plane.

"Yeah, who is it?" he called out in his deepest voice.

"It's the Archangel," the voice said.

"What?'

"Open the door, Stop," the voice said.

Carefully, he turned the handle on the door to see a man in glasses with dark wavy hair. He held a Bible in his hand. With one hand, he pushed Cotter out of the way and entered the room, closing the door behind him. "Where's the child?"

Judy raised her head from behind the couch. "In the other room sleeping. Who are you?"

"I am the Archangel," Gabriel replied. "I came to make your marriage official in the eyes of the Lord."

"Say what?" Judy and Cotter said in unison.

"I am also here to baptize the child," Gabriel said. "Please fetch her for me."

"Hold on there, buddy," Judy said, stepping forward, but the look Gabriel gave her halted her in her tracks.

Gabriel removed his glasses. "Forging a document is one thing. Lying to God is another. I traveled all the way to Vegas to make this marriage viable in the eyes of the Lord. Please don't waste my time. Do as I ask."

Cotter shooed her to fetch a sleeping Johnnie, and she returned with the sleeping girl in her arms. Shoving his weapon in his waistband, Cotter took the child from her arms and presented the sleeping angel to Gabriel. A small vial of water came from his black jacket, dabbing several drops on her forehead, sealing each drop with a kiss, and saying a prayer over her sleeping form and making the sign of the cross into her skin.

"You can take her back to bed now," Gabriel said to Judy.

Judy complied, taking Johnnie back to the room and tucking her into bed. She joined Cotter in the living room, who stood next to Gabriel, she noted who was indeed a very handsome man who wore a wedding ring.

"Stand next to your husband," Gabriel said as he opened his Bible and read a scripture. "Take her hand, Cotter."

He said the words they both had heard many times before in movies, Judy having heard them herself. This time, the words felt different. Permanent.

"What God has joined together, let no man put asunder," Gabriel said. "By the power vested in me, I pronounce you man and wife. You may kiss your bride."

Gabriel, extracting his phone from his pocket, pressed a few buttons for the Bridal March, then looked at Cotter with half a smile.

"That will be $50," Gabriel said.

"Get the hell out of here!" Cotter replied, frowning a him. "I just paid you five grand for the two documents."

"Yes, you paid for the documents, and now you have to pay me for the service," he told the man. "You are lucky I don't make you pay for my plane ticket and flowers for my very pissed off wife."

"Thank you, Archangel," Judy said shaking the large warm hand of the clergyman. "Will you bless our marriage with a prayer before you leave?"

"I wouldn't have it any other way," Gabriel said, asking them both to bow their heads.

He said a prayer of understanding and faith, dabbing both of their heads with oil as an anointment. Cotter begrudgingly paid him the $50 and Judy threw in a 20 for the flowers for his wife. She also kissed his cheek, which Cotter didn't appreciate.

"Ain't no need to kiss him," Cotter growled, frowning again at Gabriel, but more at himself. A surge of jealousy went through him seeing Judy's lips touch the good-looking man's cheek. He'd never met the man in person and always assumed he was an old bastard with gray hair, not a vibrant, very heterosexual man.

"He flew all this way to make sure we were right with God," Judy said. "Can I also buy you dinner?"

"Nope, flying home soon as I get to the airport," Gabriel said. "Blessings to you both."

He left, leaving the scent of his cologne in the room which seemed a bit vacant without his presence. Judy and Cotter both laughed. Placing her hand into his, he led her to the bedroom where they disrobed and climbed into bed.

"Judy, have you noticed that since we've been here, you haven't coughed much?"

"I noticed," she said, snuggling close to him to find that sweet spot of connection.

"You know what that means right?"

"No, husband, what does it mean?" she asked, placing a light kiss on the hairy chest.

"It means you are well enough to wear my ass out," he said chuckling.

"I guess it does at that," she said, slipping her hand deep under the covers to find he was ready for the party. "Cotter, call me stupid, but I have fallen in love you with you. I don't know if it's because you saved my life or because of you I have hope to really live one."

"I love you too, and Johnnie," he said.

"I know you do," she told him as she shifted her weight and lay her body on top of his. Slowly they made love until she increased the pace, turning the sweet lovemaking into a no holds barred scene from a porn movie. He found himself biting into the pillow at the passionate ending, holding her close as he caught his breath.

"I'm yours," he whispered into her ear.

"Yes, you are all mine," Judy said, clinging to his body.

He would sleep that night like a newborn. A happily married man and a father of one. The elusive thing he never thought he'd master, he had. He'd been honest with a woman and the whole world didn't fall apart for him telling the truth.

*I deserve this.*

*I earned this.*

*I earned them.*

He was uncertain if he would ever return to work, or if he would take sporadic jobs here or there, but his hunting days for two-legged prey had come to an end. Cotter Wihlborg was going to live an honest life as husband and father on a little spread in Rocheport, Missouri in a handmade house lit by solar power.

For the first time in his life, he couldn't wait to go home.

OLIVIA GAINES

- Fin -

# Blind Luck

FROM THE BEST SELLING AUTHOR OF BLIND DATE

OLIVIA GAINES

BLIND LUCK

ALL HE WANTED WAS BOWL OF GRITS, THREE STRIPS OF CRIPSY BACON AND CUP OF COFFEE...

Pre-Order and prepare for reading bliss.

# BLIND LUCK

The Technicians Series – Book 3

**MAY 2019**

DAVONSHIRE HOUSE PUBLISHING
Augusta, Georgia

# OLIVIA GAINES

# Chapter One - Dammit...

His leg throbbed like a son of a bitch and the oatmeal Judy had given him for breakfast was gone. His stomach ached as if he'd been punched in it with a large hammer, making the bag of goop processor feel as if someone had drained it of all it's juices. Even his bile wanted a thing or two to digest. He could taste the bitter in his mouth.

Hunger makes a man do dumb things, and he was about to do the dumbest – have a meal in a Waffle House at 3 am in the morning off a lone stretch of interstate. A lonely yellow sign stood out against the black sky. The ebony letters, half faded from spending too much time in the mid-day sun, making the trademark sign spell *Wafle Hose*, if read from left to right, since the other letters in the name had faded. He didn't care. A hot cup of coffee, a bowl of grits and maybe a couple of crisp strips of bacon would tie him over.

Mr. Yield maneuvered his Ford F-150 to the exit ramp, making the left, and driving across the interstate bridge, pulling reluctantly into the parking lot. Only three cars were in the lot. One, he assumed belonged to the night manager, the other to the waitress who as going to have entirely too much attitude for this time of morning and the third to a lonely, lone customer.

"Dammit," he mumbled as his phone began to vibrate. A call at 3 am was never good for him or the person on the other end.

"Yield," he said into the line. He knew it was Beauty Kurtzwilde and he didn't want to talk to her.

"Good morning; where are you?" She asked in the line.

"Waffle House, jut outside of St. Louis," Yield mumbled, adjusting the aching leg.

"Did you retrieve the package from Caleb Morrow's widow?"

"Yep, burned it," he lied. She didn't have the package, or at least that's what Stop had told him. He believed the man although the woman truck him as being a little on the left side of shady. That man was going to have his hands full with the woman and child. Yield saw no reason to out the man to Beauty on his change in life situation, especially since he'd done him a solid and only shot him in the leg versus kill him.

"Are you ready to for another?" Beauty asked.

"Another what?"

"A young man by the name of Luther Pennington has taken a watch that belongs to his grandfather," Beauty said. "He lives nearby in Wentzville. Are you close to that location?"

Yield looked at his GPS. He actually sat in the parking lot of the Waffle House in Wentzville. The thought of getting a hotel room for the night sat well with him, which would give him a chance to put the leg up while he slept. The dull throb from Stop digging the bullet out of his muscle and sewing him back up hurt like a moferker.

"I'll look into," he told her, "send a photo."

"No bloodshed if you can help it. The contract only requires the return of the item," Beauty said. "The originator wants help for the grandson, not death."

"Duly noted," Yield mumbled, ending the call. In a few moments an image of the young man would come through and, in the morning, he would begin his skip trace. At this moment, his belly reminded him of a couple of those crisp strips of bacon, a hot cup of black coffee and bowl of grits with cheddar cheese on top.

He cut the engine to the truck, climbing out slowly, ensuring he had his piece in his jacket pocket along with a new knife. The one he'd used to cut Stop had fallen in the snow. The knife didn't mean enough to him to go back and look for it. In his line of work, he had plenty of knives, guns, and surveillance equipment to last him a life time. Moving slowly, the bell on the glass door jangled when he opened it, stepping inside to the warmth and grease filled air.

"Morning," a pretty young woman called from behind the counter. Large brown eyes focused on his face. He knew the scar which emblazoned across his left eye and down his cheek was a turn off to a lot of women. Others found it to be a turn on, as if the scar gave him an edgy look which made him seem suspect. However, her eyes, went from his face to the man at the end of the far counter, seated in a corner with his head down.

Yield turned slowly, looking at the man who sat silently, his right leg bouncing up and down like a junkie in need of a fix. Probably going to try and rob the place. Dammit.

"Coffee, black and hot. Bacon and a bowl of grits with some cheese on top," he said, dragging the leg a bit as he went to find a seat facing the door. Wanting the last booth in the rom of three, he went to sit, but found the seat occupied by a small, sleeping, little person.

"Sorry about that," the waitress said. "Chad is sleep down there. Babysitters are so hard to come by nowadays. My Ma, won't watch him while I work, at the late shift ain't got many customers. It works out."

He said nothing. His eyes on the shifty character and then the child. A moment of envy went through him as he thought about Stop, being at the raggedy home made house with Judy and the child. A family. He wanted a family, but it would be just his dumb luck to marry a crazy bitch that liked to fight all the time. The last one gave him the ugly scar across his face.

A ping from his pocket indicated Beauty had sent the photo for his next assignment.

"Pull one bacon," the waitress yelled as a man, big around the middle, waddled from the back. The swinging door complaining of his girth as he walked over to he fridge. Grubby hands reach for the handle to pull out three strips of bacon.

"Hey, wash your hands before you touch my food," Yield said aloud.

"The heat from the grill will kill any germs," the cook grumbled.

"Either way, I would rather not have the germs from your ass on my meal," Yield said, looking down at the photo.

This was the part of his job he hated most. The images people sent of the targets were also good pics before the subject went bad. A good looking kid with blonde hair, bright blue eyes and an award winning smile looked back at him. He was pretty sure the kid didn't look like this now. If he was using, more than likely, he would look more like the kid at the end of the counter. Used up.

"Here's our coffee Mister," the young woman said, sitting the cup down. "Let me get your grits. I made them myself. Just a little bit of milk, a bit of sugar and heavy cream. Makes them grits real smooth when you stir'em up."

He watched her firm backside, young supple skin and pert breast as she leaned over the table to place the bowl in front of him. Her lips moves slowly so he could understand her words. *He's scaring me.*

Yield mouthed back, *call the cops.*

She pressed her lips together, shaking her head no. Her eyes went to the child then back to him.

Yield turned up his lip in a frown. He didn't understand what she was trying to tell him and really didn't give a shit. His leg hurt. He wanted his grits and that bacteria bacon the shit stain on life was cooking under the heavy metal press on the grill. Shrugging and reaching for the bowl, his attempt to blow her off didn't work.

Two loaded spoonful bites into his grits, Yield knew without a reasonable doubt, they were by far the best tasting boiled grounds of corn he'd ever eaten in his life. For that reason alone, he took a little more interest in what she was trying to say to him. Craning his neck, he looked over his shoulder into the seat to see the sleeping child. The child was the key to her message.

"Dammit," he mumbled out loud.

The shaky fellow looked up at him, with blue eyes and dirty blonde hair. Cursing under his breath, it was just his blind luck that the skip trace he'd been sent to retrieve was in the same hole on the same wall as him.

"Fuck it, I'm finishing my meal first," Yield said licking his lips when the bacon arrived.

"Luther, pay up or get out," the cook told the boy.

"Jake, you know I'm good for it," Luther, the shaky man said.

"Your Grandpa is good for it, you aren't good for nuthin'," the cook said feeling proud that he could lord this over the downfallen young man.

Yield hated bullies. Especially when it came to those less fortunate than others. Life had kicked the young man hard in the teeth, and this ass wipe wasn't helping.

"Luther," he said aloud. "You hungry?'

"Yeah, but I ain't got no money," he said.

"I'll buy anything you have on you that's worth a twenty so you can get yourself a meal," Yield said to the young man.

"All I have is this watch, and I can't sell it for no twenty damned bucks," Luther said.

"What do you want for it?"

"A hundred! A hundred dollars," Luther said.

"Deal," Yield said. "Hand the watch to Millicent over here, who will bring it to me and carry back the hundred. Easy transaction. You get a meal, the cook is happy, I get a watch and Millicent earns a nice tip."

A shaky Luther gawked at him. The once nice teeth as shown on the photo on his phone were now black from smoking meth. The smooth, well cared for skin in the photo was pock marked and full in sores.

"No funny stuff out you Mister," Luther challenged.

"I'm not going to move which is why the sweet Millicent is going to bring you over this bill," he said, taking a crisp note from his wallet. "You hand her the watch she hands you the bill and everyone is good."

"What if I keep the watch and your bill then kick your ass?" Luther asked, feeling bold.

"Then, your Grandfather is going to be real pissed at me when I return that watch to him and put a bullet in you," Yield growled out.

Millicent jumped, the cook dropped the spatula and Luther's eyes grew wide. Yield loved this portion of the job. He called it the 'come to Jesus' moment.

"Yep, your Grandpa sent me to get his watch back," Yield said. "Normally, I would kick your ass and take back the stolen property, because that's what I enjoy doing. But this morning, I'm tired. My leg hurts, I'm sleepy and a bit pissed off. However, Millicent here has made me feel kindly towards you after eating this bowl of yumminess. So do all of us a favor, take the damned money, give me the fucking watch and for God's sake, eat some food!"

He handed Millicent the bill which she accepted with shaking hands. Hesitantly she moved down the walkway behind the counter to Luther, who pulled the watch from his pocket. Tears filled his eyes as he handed it to the young waitress, who put it in her pocket then handed him the bill.

"Come to me Millicent," Yield said, holding a strip of bacon in his hand. "Cook, make the man a steak with a side of eggs and put it on my tab."

She reached his booth, passing him the watch. He stared at the inanimate object. The old man wanted it back, more than likely as a last straw to take one more thing from the kid. It wasn't his business.

"Thanks," he said to Millicent, sliding the watch into his pocket.

Her eyes going to the child.

"Are you going to be in town for a while?" She asked, wanting to ask him for help that he didn't fucking feel like giving.

"Nope," he replied. The way the hope drained from her face said it all. The kid's father was an asshole. *A local cop?* "Whaddya need?"

He couldn't believe he'd said the words.

"A ride home would be nice for me and my kid," she said. "You can have the couch to sleep on tonight, if you want. It's lumpy, but it sure beats you staying in the local motel. It's safer too."

"And what if I'm jut going to keep rolling?"

"You can't," she said turning her back to him to get the him a refresh on his coffee. "Mr. Pennington lives twenty miles outside of town, and your bandage is bleeding on your leg."

"Fuck," he mumbled; she was right. His leg had started to bleed.

"No, that's not on the table, but Mister, it sure does sound good," she said with a wink.

*How do I get myself into shit like this was the first thing that went through my head. The second thing was the possibility of a good fuck from a young pretty thing like her with lots of energy. Hurt leg or not, I could just hold tight and let her do the work. A third thing popped into my head as well. The kid.*

It always starts with the damned kid.

MILLICENT ST. JAMES lived in a trailer park, just inside the city limits of Wentzville, Missouri. The sparse place was clean, the kitchen sink empty of dirty dishes and the fridge full of Waffle House to-go containers. He surmised it was how she and the kid ate on the regular.

"What's the story? The boy's Pap is a cop?" He asked, taking a seat in one of the two kitchen chairs.

"No," she said. "His Uncle is the cop. Chad's father is his brother," she said. "You know the type, never wanting to help but always want to make the rules of what I can and can't do. *You're a bad Mom* sort of shit, while he's down in St. Louis laid up with a chick with big fake titties and fat injected into her ass."

"May be some merit to it, you bringing home strangers and all for a ride," he said it with a double-edged meaning.

"I said you could sleep in the couch," she told him.

"You also said a fuck would be nice," Yield said. "I gave you the lift home with hopes that once my leg got bandaged, you would come through. I'm a man, that's how I think. Women don't think like us, you folks are always planning, six steps ahead of our sluggish brains. What are you hoping to get out of the deal?"

"Truthfully?"

"Why not? Lying don't get you very far with me," he said.

"Shit, I'm hoping, if I am to be honest," she said, biting her bottom lip, "that if I fuck you good enough, that you will take me and the kid with you."

"Lady, you don't know me!"

"I sure as hell don't which should make you really wonder, how completely awful my life must be here if I'm asking to go with you!" Millicent said.

"Yeah, but where am I taking you?"

"To your house," she said. "I am a great housekeeper, a fantastic cook, and Chad won't be a problem. It's just for a little while until we can figure out what's next. If not, and you leave me here, life is just going to get uglier for us. Help me. Help my child. Help us get a new life."

"What if I'm married and got a woman?"

"Do you?"

"Hell no," he said.

"Then good, I can be your woman for a while," she said, getting the first aid kit. "But first, let me take care of that leg."

"I can do it," he said. "Plus, I would have to take off my pants."

"Well, Mister, I sure as hell can't fuck you with them on," Millicent offered.

- Fin-

Coming May 2019. You can pre-order by clicking here[1] on Amazon or here for other platforms https://books2read.com/u/3JyK8P

---

1. https://www.amazon.com/dp/B07MQVPDZT

# About the Author

AS A MULTIPLE AWARD-winning, best-selling Amazon author, Olivia loves a good laugh coupled with some steam, mixed in with a man and woman finding their way past the words of "I love you." An author of contemporary romances, she writes heartwarming stories of blossoming relationships about couples not only falling in love but building a life after the hot sex scene. When Olivia is not writing, she enjoys quilting, playing Scrabble online against other word lovers and spending time with her family. She is an avid world traveler who writes many of the locations into her stories. Most of the time she can be found sitting quietly with pen and paper plotting more adventures in love. Olivia lives in Hephzibah, Georgia with her husband, son, grandson and snotty evil cat, Katness Evermean.

Learn more about her books, upcoming releases and join her bibliophile nation at www.ogaines.com[1]

Subscribe to her email list at http://eepurl.com/OuIYf

Facebook: https://www.facebook.com/olivia.gaines.31

Twitter: https://twitter.com/oliviagaines

---

1. https://l.facebook.com/
   l.php?u=http%3A%2F%2Fwww.ogaines.com%2F&h=ATM0gHv0hj4DZhvKKKKqUE77XlcEzrn-
   VH_6xve-RzPYCe2ddOeY7Ld6q8EK2KB6G2-Zc7CUvUzJL9MMmQeEiMaEj1jwnFtyQPaggbrN-
   J182tnDtcE4ZLlVvjqvUbVXPL8Tr2Q

Instagram: https://www.instagram.com/gaines.olivia/

# Don't miss out!

Visit the website below and you can sign up to receive emails whenever Olivia Gaines publishes a new book. There's no charge and no obligation.

https://books2read.com/r/B-A-KVAB-RHKX

**BOOKS 2 READ**

Connecting independent readers to independent writers.

Did you love *Blind Hope*? Then you should read *Blind Date* by Olivia Gaines!

The Man was given an assignment- to take care of Shanice Olleh. However, he never expected to find a child or the woman he sent to handle, be so attractive. Making a call which could end his career or his life, he forever alters Shanice's life after one blind date.Shanice Olleh agrees to a blind date with her boss's friend, but the evening shifts when a hired hit man takes an interest in his mark.Welcome back to Venture, Georgia with this dark romance, and loving a bad guy, being so good.

Read more at ogaines.com.

# Also by Olivia Gaines

**Modern Mail Order Brides**
On A Rainy Night in Georgia
Buckeye and the Babe
The Tennessee Mountain Man
Bleu, Grass, Bourbon

**Prado Sloe Investigators**
Prado Sloe: The Case of the Merger
Prado Sloe and the Case of the Merger

**Serenity Series**
Welcome to Serenity
Holden
Farmer Takes A Wife

**Slice of Life**
Friends with Benefits

**Slivers of Love**

The Cost to Play
Thursdays in Savannah
The Deal Breaker

**The Blakemore Files**
Being Mrs. Blakemore
Shopping with Mrs. Blakemore
Dancing with Mr. Blakemore
Cruising with the Blakemores
Dinner with the Blakemores
Loving the Czar
Being Mr. Blakemore
A Weekend with the Blakemores

**The Davonshire Series**
Courting Guinevere

**The Men of Endurance**
A Walk Through Endurance
Intervals of Love
The Art of Persistence
A Walk Through Endurance

**The Technicians**
Blind Hope
Blind Luck

Watch for more at ogaines.com.

Made in the USA
Columbia, SC
26 March 2020